Cody was about to fold up her map when she spotted two more pairs of letters at the bottom of the page. Next to them was another question mark.

"What about these?" she asked the others, pointing to them. "'Au' and 'Ag.'"

"Auto?" M.E. guessed, wrinkling her nose.

"Agate?" Luke said. "Although that makes about as much sense as 'auto.'"

M.E. elbowed him playfully in the ribs.

"I think we were right the first time with *this* one," Quinn said, one eyebrow raised mysteriously. "On the periodic table, 'Au' is the symbol for gold, and 'Ag' is the symbol for silver."

THE CODE BUSTERS CLUB

CASE #1
The Secret of the Skeleton Key

CASE #2
The Haunted Lighthouse

CASE #4
The Mummy's Curse

The
CODE BUSTERS
CLUB

CASE #3:

The Mystery of the
Pirate's Treasure

Penny Warner

EGMONT
USA
New York

EGMONT

We bring stories to life

First published by Egmont USA, 2013
This paperback edition published by Egmont USA, 2014
443 Park Avenue South, Suite 806
New York, NY 10016

1 3 5 7 9 8 6 4 2

www.egmontusa.com
www.pennywarner.com
www.CodeBustersClub.com

THE LIBRARY OF CONGRESS HAS CATALOGED
THE HARDCOVER EDITION AS FOLLOWS:

Warner, Penny.
Mystery of the pirate's treasure / by Penny Warner.
pages cm. — (The Code Busters Club ; case #3)
Summary: When the Code Busters visit the Carmel Mission, a series of coded
messages sets them on the hunt for long hidden pirate treasure.
ISBN 978-1-60684-457-1 (hardcover) — ISBN 978-1-60684-458-8 (ebook)
[1. Cryptography--Fiction. 2. Ciphers—Fiction. 3. School field trips—Fiction. 4. Mission
San Carlos Borromeo (Carmel, Calif.)—Fiction. 5. Bouchard, Hippolyte—Fiction. 6.
Pirates—Fiction. 7. Buried treasure—Fiction. 8. Mystery and dectective stories.] I. Title.
PZ7.W2458Myp 2013
[Fic]--dc23
2012045855

Paperback ISBN 978-1-60684-517-2
Printed in the United States of America

To my treasure hunters: Bradley,
Stephanie, Luke, and Lyla

READER

To see keys and solutions to the puzzles inside, go to the Code Buster's Key Book & Solutions on page 165.

To see complete Code Busters Club Rules and Dossiers, and solve more puzzles and mysteries, go to **www.CodeBustersClub.com**

CODE BUSTERS CLUB RULES

Motto
To solve puzzles, codes, and mysteries and
keep the Code Busters Club secret!

Secret Sign
Interlocking index fingers
(American Sign Language sign for "friend")

Secret Password
Day of the week, said backward

Secret Meeting Place
Code Busters Club Clubhouse

Code Busters Club Dossiers

IDENTITY: Quinn Kee

Code Name: "Lock&Key"

Description
Hair: Black, spiky
Eyes: Brown
Other: Sunglasses

Special Skill: Video games, Computers, Guitar

Message Center: Doghouse

Career Plan: CIA cryptographer
or Game designer

Code Specialties: Military code,
Computer codes

IDENTITY: MariaElena—M.E.—Esperanto

Code Name: "Em-me"

Description
Hair: Long, brown
Eyes: Brown
Other: Fab clothes

Special Skill: Handwriting analysis, Fashionista

Message Center: Flower box

Career Plan: FBI handwriting analyst or Veterinarian

Code Specialties: Spanish, I.M., Text messaging

IDENTITY: Luke LaVeau

Code Name: "Kuel-Dude"

Description
Hair: Black, curly
Eyes: Dark brown
Other: Saints cap

Special Skill: Extreme sports, Skateboard, Crosswords

Message Center: Under step

Career Plan: Pro skater, Stuntman, Race car driver

Code Specialties: Word puzzles, Skater slang

IDENTITY: Dakota—Cody—Jones

Code Name: "CodeRed"

Description
Hair: Red, curly
Eyes: Green
Other: Freckles

Special Skill: Languages,
Reading faces and body language

Message Center: Tree knothole

Career Plan: Interpreter for UN or deaf people

Code Specialties: Sign language,
Braille, Morse code, Police codes

CONTENTS*

To crack the chapter title code, check out the CODE BUSTER'S Key Book & Solutions on pages 169 and 178.

Chapter 1

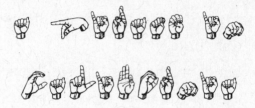

S tudents, your attention, please," Ms. Stadelhofer announced to her sixth-grade class. "Do any of you recognize this book?"

Dakota—Cody—Jones was about to raise her hand to answer when Matt the Brat, the kid who sat in front of her, turned around in his seat.

"Is that your baby book, Cody-Toady?" Matt teased. His breath smelled of peanut butter.

Cody glared at him.

"Matthew Jeffreys, turn around and pay attention," Ms. Stad said sharply.

"Sorry, Stad . . . I mean, Ms. Stadelhofer," Matt said.

Cody could tell that he didn't mean a word of his apology.

Ms. Stadelhofer held up the book again. "How many of you learned Mother Goose nursery rhymes when you were little?"

All the hands in the class shot up—except one: Matt the Brat's. He'd never admit to knowing such babyish stories.

"Do any of you remember this rhyme?" Stad asked. She began to read from the large picture book:

"*Sing a song of sixpence*
"*A pocket full of rye . . .*"

Cody's best friend, M.E.—MariaElena Esperanto—waved her hand. Cody knew M.E. loved poetry. It wasn't surprising she'd know nursery rhymes.

"Yes, MariaElena?" said Ms. Stad.

"My *tía* used to sing that to me every night at bedtime," M.E. said proudly. "I know the whole thing by heart."

"Would you like to recite it for us?" Ms. Stad asked.

M.E. stood up by her desk and cleared her throat as if she were about to sing an opera.

"Sing a song of sixpence
"A pocket full of rye
"Four and twenty blackbirds
"Baked in a pie.
"When the pie was opened
"The birds began to sing
"Was that not a tasty dish
"To set before a king?"

The class burst into applause.

"Nice job, MariaElena," Ms. Stad said. "Now, do

3

you know what the rhyme means?"

M.E. frowned. "Uh . . . somebody baked a pie full of birds for the king? Sounds yucky to me."

Everyone laughed.

"Believe it or not," Ms. Stad said, after the laughter died down, "many of the nursery rhymes are actually about real historical events and have secret meanings."

Cody's ears pricked up.

"Sometimes the rhymes made fun of the royal family or the political events of the day," Ms. Stad continued. "Commoners didn't have free speech back then, like we do today. If they criticized the government, they could have been arrested, or worse."

Cody shivered. Imagine being arrested—or worse—for just talking.

"Many of the coded references in the rhymes are about wars, plagues, and injustice. Most people didn't read or write, so they memorized rhymes. Believe it or not, even pirates used rhymes to pass on secret messages."

"Pirates?" Matt the Brat blurted, forgetting to

raise his hand. Ms. Stad shot him a warning look. Quickly, he held up his hand, then bent it into the shape of a hook and added, "Arrg!"

Cody could just picture Matt wearing an eye patch and swinging a sword—right before he tripped and fell off the gangplank into crocodile-infested waters. She smiled at the image.

But the word *pirate* had definitely caught Cody's attention, too. Cody loved adventures and had read everything from *Treasure Island* and *Robinson Crusoe* to *Island of the Blue Dolphins* and *Little House on the Prairie.*

As Ms. Stad gave Matt her usual lecture about staying focused and using good manners, Cody jotted down a coded note for M.E. using her Caesar's cipher wheel. M.E. and Cody were members of the Code Busters Club, along with Quinn Kee and Luke LaVeau from Mr. Pike's class. They'd formed the club because they all loved creating and cracking codes, and they had built their own clubhouse in a nearby eucalyptus forest. The four kids had made their own ciphers by cutting out two circles, one larger than the other. They'd written the alphabet around the edge of the outer circle, and then they'd done the same on the rim of the inner circle but had mixed up the letters. It was one of Cody's favorite ways of sending secret messages. After lining up the letter Z on the inner circle with the letter A on the outer circle, Cody quickly coded the message by substituting the corresponding letters. That way no one could read it if it fell into the wrong hands—like Matt the Brat's.

She located the first letter of her message on the outer circle—*I*—then wrote down the corresponding letter underneath it—*X*. She continued to code each letter until the sentence was complete:

X HBRVDC XP UJDCD'I Z KXCZUD LBVD?

Code Buster's Key and Solution found on pp. 168, 172.

Using origami, Cody folded the sheet of binder paper into a hidden square within a square, with the message inside. She passed the palm-sized note to Becca behind her, who passed it to Susan, who passed it to Lyla, who passed it to Stephanie, who passed it to M.E.

"Quiet down, please," said Ms. Stad, calling the

buzzing students back to attention. "You might be surprised to learn that the nursery rhyme 'Sing a Song of Sixpence' was actually a message that pirates used to recruit crew members for their ships. 'Sing a song of sixpence' refers to the amount of money the pirates would earn for the trip. 'A pocket full of rye' is about how they spent their money. 'Four and twenty blackbirds baked in a pie' meant the pirates planned to lure other ships in range, then launch a surprise attack. 'When the pie was opened' meant the attack itself, and 'the birds began to sing' was about the pirates who fought in the attack."

Ms. Stad paused for a moment, looking out at her students, who were mesmerized by her story. She grinned. "Can anyone guess who 'the king' refers to?"

A few hands went up. "The king of England?" asked Bradley in the back row.

"No," said Ms. Stadelhofer.

"The king of Spain?" asked Jodie.

Ms. Stad shook her head.

Hands slowly went down. "Give up?" she asked. The students nodded. "Actually, 'the king' doesn't refer to a real king at all. It refers to Blackbeard the Pirate!"

"*Cool, too bad there aren't any pirates like Blackbeard anymore*, Cody thought.

"Class," Ms. Stad said. "I have a special 'pie' of my own to share with you. But this will be a good surprise."

Everyone sat quietly, waiting. Cody wondered what it could be. A Pirate Day in the classroom? A lesson on how to talk like a pirate? Or maybe Ms. Stad planned to teach them a *real* pirate code?

"Did you find an envelope inside your backpacks yesterday?" Ms. Stad asked.

Cody nodded and noticed the other students nodding as well.

"What was inside?" Ms. Stad asked.

Hands shot up. Ms. Stad called on Becca.

"There was a long, rectangular piece of paper shaped like a mission building," she answered, "with small windows and a bell tower."

"Was anything written on the paper?"

"No, it was blank," answered Bradley.

"Was there anything else in the envelope?"

"Yeah," answered Lyla. "A pen, but I think the ink was dried up. I tried to write with it, and there was nothing there."

Cody's hand went up. "It was an invisible-ink decoder pen. If you colored over the paper, a bunch of letters showed up."

Ms. Stad held up a larger version of the grid:

C	P	I	R	A	T	E	S	A	M
A	B	C	D	E	F	G	E	H	I
R	I	J	V	K	L	M	A	N	S
M	O	P	I	W	H	E	R	E	S
E	Q	R	S	S	T	U	C	V	I
L	W	X	I	Y	Z	A	H	B	O
W	A	N	T	S	C	D	E	E	N
H	F	F	G	H	I	J	D	K	L
O	O	M	N	T	H	E	O	P	Q
T	R	E	A	S	U	R	E	R	S

Code Buster's Solution found on p. 172.

"Duh," said Matt. "I did that, but the letters didn't make any sense."

"It was a puzzle," M.E. said. "Like a hidden-word search. You had to solve it to figure it out."

"She's right," Ms. Stad said. "There are words hidden in the grid. They run horizontally, vertically, and even diagonally. They relate to a theme."

Cody and her friends had quickly figured out what kind of puzzle it was when they'd found it. They made puzzles like this for one another all the time. Five of the hidden words jumped out at Cody immediately—the ones along the edges of the puzzle. The Code Busters had circled the words when they spotted them, then written them all down. Soon they had a list of twelve random words. All of the leftover letters—the ones not circled—were in alphabetical order.

Ms. Stad went to the whiteboard. "All right, class. Those of you who found the hidden words, please raise your hands and I'll call on you to share them." Stad wrote down the words as they were called out.

"It still doesn't make any sense," Matt argued.

"It's just a bunch of random words."

Cody raised her hand. "It's a word anagram," she said. "You have to rearrange the words in order to make a sentence."

"Right, again!" Ms. Stad said. "So which word comes first?"

"Who!" called out Stephanie.

"Raise your hands, please," Ms. Stad reminded the class. She wrote the word *Who* on the board. Once the words were placed in order and the puzzle was solved, Ms. Stad read the sentence out loud.

"Awesome!" Bradley said. "I love searching for pirate's treasure. This is going to be totally fun."

Matt the Brat turned and frowned. "Dude, there's no such thing as hidden treasure in California. They only find that kind of stuff at the bottom of the sea."

Ms. Stad grinned at the class. "I guess we'll find out soon enough. As you know, we've been studying our state's history and the settling of the American West. We've also just learned about mapping. We may not have the battlefields of the South or the fishing ports of the Northeast, the pioneer trails of the

Midwest, or even the pirates along the East Coast. But we do have our unique California missions— you learned about them in fourth grade—and we'll be taking a field trip to the Carmel Mission. There, you'll learn about mission life in the 1700s and visit the tiny room where Junipero Serra, founder of the mission, lived. Father Serra helped explore and colonize the area that became our home state, California."

The class cheered at the idea of a field trip. But Cody felt a little disappointed. The Carmel Mission? It was hardly Gettysburg or Plymouth Rock or even the Smithsonian Institution in Washington, D.C.— places she'd always wanted to see, where history really came alive.

Ms. Stad seemed to read her thoughts. "You'll be seeing real California history on this trip, class. The missions are among the oldest buildings in the state, constructed between 1769 and 1833. If it weren't for the missions, we might not be here today. Each mission was built thirty miles away from the last—a day on horseback, three days on foot—so that travelers

12

could stop, rest, and have a meal before moving on to the next mission."

Cody couldn't imagine walking three days from one place to the next. Things had really changed.

Ms. Stad rang a bell to get the students' attention again.

"Bells were important back in the mission days. They were rung at mealtime, as calls to religious services, during births, and at funerals. Bells were also rung to warn people of danger. One of your assignments during our trip will be to identify all the mission bells you can."

Cool, Cody thought. This *would* be like a treasure hunt. She wondered what other kinds of bell codes there were. Maybe the Code Busters could make their own. One bell for "Listen!" Two bells for "Come quick!" Three bells for "Danger!" Ms. Stad rang the bell again to quiet the kids. "Also, we'll be camping overnight and hiking the Mission Trail Nature Preserve."

More cheers from the students.

"And that's not all. Matt, you said there were no

pirates and no buried treasure in California. But that's not true. We *do* have one pirate—the only known pirate in California. His name was Hippolyte de Bouchard. He and his men landed in the Monterey Bay to search for treasure that was rumored to have been hidden by the missionaries!"

A pirate named Hippolyte? Cody thought. *A hidden treasure at a mission? An overnight field trip? A hunt for mission bells? This is going to be awesome!*

Chapter 2

After school, Cody and M.E. headed for the Code Busters Clubhouse. The girls trudged up the hillside talking excitedly about the upcoming field trip to the Carmel Mission.

"I've never been to Carmel before," M.E. said, her long dark braid swinging down her back as she walked. Dressed in pink jeans, a Tinkerbell T-shirt, and rhinestone-embellished flip-flops, she looked out of place among the thick foliage and towering trees. But then, so did Cody in her jeans, blue T-shirt, and red Chuck Taylors. Luckily, the fall weather was still mild, even in the shadowed forest. And at least Cody had on shoes that gripped the slippery, needle-laden path, instead of M.E.'s slippery flip-flops.

"My mom and I went to Carmel a few weekends ago to visit my aunt Abigail," Cody said. "She lives in this little cottage with seven cats. It reminds me of 'Snow White and the Seven Dwarfs.' She took us to the Monterey Bay Aquarium, where we saw a bunch of sharks. Pretty awesome."

"I love aquariums!" said M.E., who got excited about almost everything. "I wish we could go there on the field trip. I want to see the penguins and the stingrays and the eels and the octopuses."

"I think it's *octopi*," Cody said, correcting her.

"I hope there aren't any mountain lions at the campsite," M.E. said, glancing nervously behind her and quickening her step. Cody sped up to keep pace with M.E. The girls had never actually seen a mountain lion in the eucalyptus forest, but others had spotted the big cat, so they were always on alert.

Moments later they reached the clubhouse. The original building had been destroyed by an evil pair of crooks who had tried to steal from Cody's neighbor, but the Code Busters had rebuilt it out of torn-down billboards, wood planks, and a camouflage parachute they'd bought at the army-navy supply store. Cody glanced around to make sure no one had followed them. She knew Luke LaVeau and Quinn Kee, the other two club members, were already there, because the outside lock was open. Then she gave the secret knock, tapping out two letters in Morse code:

-.. .---

M.E. did the same:

-- .

Code Buster's Key and Solution found on pp. 166, 173.

Once they'd tapped out their initials, they leaned in and said the secret word of the day: "Yadnom," which wasn't very easy to say. But then, it wasn't easy to say any of the days of the week backward.

Code Buster's Solution found on p. 173.

Cody heard the wooden two-by-four scrape across the inside of the paneled door. Someone was lifting the bar that blocked the entrance. Seconds later, the clubhouse door swung open.

"About time," Quinn said, backing up to allow the girls to enter the tiny room. He checked his military watch to stress his point.

Cody shrugged. "We're sorry, guys. We would have been here sooner, but Stad kept M.E. after class for passing notes."

M.E. rolled her eyes. "Yeah, thanks, Cody."

Cody smiled guiltily as she set down her backpack and sat on the cool sheet metal floor. The kids kept their treasures—night goggles, flashlights, and other gear—hidden underneath the floor. Soft light filtered in through the translucent parachute roof.

The others joined her on the floor, sitting cross-legged, almost knee to knee.

"Dude," Quinn said to Cody, "are you psyched for the field trip on Friday?"

She nodded. "I love pirates. I bet there's a pirate

code we can learn before we go."

"'Hornswoggle' means cheating someone out of money or treasure and stuff," Luke said.

"Where'd you learn all that?" Quinn asked.

"Yosemite Sam cartoons," Luke replied.

Quinn and Cody laughed, but Cody noticed M.E. had a distant look in her eyes, as if she hadn't been listening. Cody sensed something was up with her friend.

"Aren't you excited about the field trip, M.E.?"

M.E. came out of her daydream and shrugged again. "I've never been away from home before without my family. At least, not overnight."

Cody frowned. This was the first time her class had gone on an overnight trip. She had to admit she was a little nervous about it, but the idea of going on an adventure excited her. "Yes you have, M.E. You spend the night at my house all the time."

"That's different," M.E. said. "Your house is only a couple of blocks away from mine. And I can go home any time I want."

"So what are you afraid of?" Luke asked. Luke,

who was always doing crazy, daring stunts on his skateboard, didn't seem to have any fears. He was always the first one to take a chance or try something new. In the short time that Cody had known him, he'd gone zip-lining, entered a haunted house, competed in extreme skateboarding competitions, and had even eaten a live bug. Cody couldn't help but admire his courage. Maybe losing his parents back in New Orleans and having to move in with his *grand-mère* had made him tougher.

"I'm not *afraid!*" M.E. argued. "I just haven't slept away from home much."

Cody put an arm around her friend. "You'll be fine. I'll be right there with you, and there will be tons of other people around. Plus, I don't think there are any mountain lions in Carmel, like there are around here."

"No mountain lions," Luke added with a grin. "Just a few sharks in the bay."

M.E. broke into a smile.

"Well, I can't wait to get on that bus at eight a.m. on Friday," Quinn said, then turned to M.E. "And we're not going without you."

Luke adjusted his New Orleans Saints cap. "Okay, now that that's settled, let's compare the maps we got in our classes and see if there are some clues to this so-called treasure our teachers were talking about."

Quinn and Luke were in a different class from Cody and M.E., but Mr. Pike and Ms. Stadelhofer used the same curriculum and had passed out maps to both classes. The Code Busters pulled out their copies from their backpacks and began studying the area that featured San Carlos Borroméo de Carmelo Mission, aka the Carmel Mission, and the Mission Trail Nature Preserve nearby.

"Check it out!" Quinn said, smoothing his rumpled map. "It actually looks like a pirate's treasure map. Pretty cool."

Cody studied her copy of the map. Quinn was right. The area was laid out like a pirate map, with strange symbols and letters in a box on the side. The only trouble was, the key had been replaced with fill-in-the-blank lines.

Code Buster's Key and Solution found on pp. 166, 173.

Quinn scratched his head. "It says at the bottom that we're supposed to decode the symbols."

Cody looked over the symbols and letter pairs next to them: ca, po, st, br, ro, ga, be, tr.

"So what do they mean?" M.E. asked, perking up at the idea of solving a code.

"That's the thing," Quinn said. "We have to figure them out."

"Where's the instruction sheet?" Luke asked, turning the paper over to see if there were any clues

22

written on the back. It was blank.

"The teachers are handing that out tomorrow," Cody said. "This is all we have right now."

Quinn got a pencil out of his backpack, along with his Case Files Codebook. "Well, this is what we Code Busters do best, so let's get to it."

"All right," said Cody, focusing on the symbols. "We know these are letters. So what do they stand for?"

"They sort of look like they're from the periodic table," M.E. suggested.

Quinn flipped over to the periodic table chart he kept in his codebook. He was a whiz at science and considered the table to be a code. Cody couldn't figure out why he needed it, since he'd already memorized the whole thing.

"Look," he said, showing the table to M.E.

M.E. leaned over. "There's 'Be' for 'beryllium,' 'Ca' for 'calcium,' and 'Ga' for something called 'gallium,' whatever that is."

"Right," Quinn agreed, "but what about st, ro, and tr? There are no elements that match those letters."

M.E.'s shoulders sank. "I don't know, then."

"Maybe we can take a clue from the chart," Cody said. "Some of these elements are coded by using the first two letters of the words, like 'Ca' for 'calcium.' We can try doing the same thing for these map letters. Maybe the first two letters stand for words."

"How about 'ca' stands for 'camp,' since those marks on the map look like little tents?" Luke offered.

Quinn wrote "camp" next to the letters "ca" on the map. "What about 'po' . . . 'poop'?"

Luke laughed.

M.E. sat up. "How about 'pool' or 'pond'?"

The others looked at the map. "I think she might be right," said Cody. "That area over there looks like a water hole with a stream running through it. I think she nailed it."

Together, the Code Busters deciphered the rest of the symbols, until they'd solved the key. At least, they hoped they'd solved it right. They'd find out when their teachers checked their answers. Cody loved that Ms. Stadelhofer made so many of their lessons a game—especially when she used codes. It made learning stuff a lot more fun.

Cody was about to fold up her map when she spotted two more pairs of letters at the bottom of the page. Next to them was another question mark. "What about these?" she asked the others, pointing to them. "'Au' and 'Ag.'"

"Auto?" M.E. guessed, wrinkling her nose.

"Agate?" Luke said. "Although that makes about as much sense as 'auto.'"

M.E. elbowed him playfully in the ribs.

"I think we were right the first time with *this* one," Quinn said, one eyebrow raised mysteriously. "On the periodic table, 'Au' is the symbol for gold, and 'Ag' is the symbol for silver."

Cody lay awake in her bed that night, staring at the map. She loved making treasure maps for her friends to follow. She filled them with twists and turns, dead ends, cryptic clues, and challenging symbols. Each time she created a map quest for the other Code Busters, she led them on a hunt through the neighborhood, often directing them with compass orientations and codes, like "Go NW, 10 paces, TR, make a UT, go L90 degrees," and so on. And she always had a "treasure" waiting for them at the end—some candy, small school items, or puzzles downloaded from the Internet.

Code Buster's Solution found on p. 173.

That night Cody dreamed of pirates and ships, treasure chests and gold coins, and mystifying maps that kept leading to dead ends. The only things missing from her dream were Peter Pan, Captain Hook, and Tinkerbell. When she woke the next morning and remembered it was only Tuesday, she thought Friday—Field Trip Day—would never come. She couldn't wait to learn more about California's only real pirate: Hippolyte de Bouchard.

Not to mention the possibility of finding hidden treasure.

Chapter 3

Friday took forever to arrive—at least in Cody's mind. The trip to Carmel was all she could think about. Her mom had bought her new pajamas (Minnie Mouse), a robe (red), and slippers (black) for the overnight stay, and a dark sleeping bag decorated with glow-in-the-dark stars.

Cody had already packed her clothes in her small suitcase and added a bunch of stuff to take with her—snacks, games, and of course her Code Busting supplies, including an invisible-ink pen, her Code Busters notebook, and a mini-flashlight/whistle/keychain she might need in an emergency. All that was left to pack was her cell phone, her mini-tablet, and her toothbrush.

M.E. arrived at her house a little past seven a.m., towing her Hello Kitty suitcase and matching sleeping bag. After the two girls listened to Mrs. Jones's lecture about safety—the same lecture she'd heard over the phone from her dad—Cody kissed her sister good-bye and they headed for school. Cody felt like running. She was that excited about the field trip. If she didn't have to drag her suitcase and sleeping bag, she probably would have.

"What did you pack?" Cody asked M.E. as they walked along the tree-lined street.

"Everything," M.E. said. "My hair bands, my lucky socks, three pairs of shoes, my sleeping kitty, my cozy blanket, my jewelry box, a first-aid kit, some candy, chips, an apple—"

"You're right," Cody said, interrupting her friend as they reached Berkeley Cooperative Middle School.

"You really did pack everything. I'm surprised you didn't bring your hamster."

"I would have, but I didn't want the bears to eat him."

"There aren't any bears in Carmel, silly. Only whales, sea otters, seals, sea lions . . ."

"And bats," M.E. added. "I heard there were lots of bats."

"Well, just don't make any high-pitched noises and they'll leave you alone," Cody teased.

The girls went to meet their classmates at the front of the school, where the bus was waiting. Most of the kids were already on board. Ms. Stad stood at the bus door, checking in students, sticking on nametags, helping stow suitcases, and looking over-whelmed, even though the trip hadn't even begun.

Cody and M.E. climbed on and headed to the back, where Quinn and Luke already sat.

"We saved you a place," Quinn said, removing his Cal-Berkeley hoodie from the seat across the aisle.

Cody and M.E. took off their backpacks and scooted in, then shoved their packs under the se

"Did you bring your notebook?" Quinn asked, adjusting the aviator sunglasses that rested on his spiky black hair. He'd dressed in a black T-shirt that read SPECIAL FX, jeans, and black-and-white-checkered Vans.

"Of course," M.E. said, clicking her seat belt over the rhinestone-studded T-shirt that matched her glittery jeans. She looked like she was going to a party, not a campsite.

Luke, wearing gold and black Saints athletic pants and a sweatshirt, leaned around Quinn to talk to the girls. "I brought a snakebite kit," he said, proudly.

Quinn turned to him and shook his head. "Dude, there aren't any poisonous snakes in Carmel, only ring-necked snakes, and they aren't dangerous. And even if you do get bitten by a poisonous snake, you probably aren't going to die. Just don't go looking under rocks and logs. That's where they like to hide."

Cody saw M.E. shiver at the mention of snakes. While M.E. loved animals, she preferred the tame ones, not the ones that might bite or eat you. Cody couldn't blame her. Death by snakebite sounded pretty awful.

Once everyone was on board, including the four parent chaperones, Ms. Stad stood at the front of the bus to make her usual announcements.

"All right, listen up, please. We're about to head out, and I want to go over a few rules."

Some of the students groaned, but most were quiet as Ms. Stad reviewed her list. They knew the sooner Ms. Stad finished her lecture, the sooner they'd be off on their adventure. After she covered the basics, she gave a little history about the Carmel Mission. Back in fourth grade, when they'd studied the missions, Cody had been a little bored. But now that they were actually going to a real mission instead of building one out of Popsicle sticks, she found herself interested.

Her thoughts were interrupted by Ms. Stad's mention of the Carmel Mission pirate.

". . . Hippolyte de Bouchard was an Argentinean ship captain who attacked several California missions, including the one in Carmel, back in 1818. Did he find the treasure he was looking for?" she asked. Hands went up, but Ms. Stad shook her head. "You'll have to wait until we get to the mission museum to find out. For now, each of you will get a sheet of instructions that goes along with the map I handed out on Monday. If you follow all the instructions, you just might discover where the treasure is—if there is one." She smiled at the end of her mysterious lecture.

The teachers and parent volunteers passed out the papers to the students. When Cody got hers, she pulled out the map Ms. Stad had given everyone earlier, and set them side by side on her lap. The instruction sheet listed a number of step-by-step directions, along with familiar-looking icons—/\ for "tent," - - - for "trail," h for "bench," H for "gate"—and one new one: # for "danger."

She glanced at the map and located the icons, then turned her attention back to the directions.

1. **Find your /\ and set up.**
2. **Gather at the beginning of the - - - .**
3. **As you walk, watch for hidden messages near each h.**

4. Gather at the H.

5. Keep an eye out for #!

Code Buster's Solution found on p. 174.

That sounded easy enough, but she wondered where, exactly, the path would lead. And what hidden messages they were supposed to find? Ms. Stad had hinted that there would be clues along the way. Cody hoped so. That would make it even more fun! Only one thing bothered her.

Why was there a # symbol?

Cody and Quinn texted each other during the nearly two-hour bus ride to Carmel. At one point, Quinn said, "Check your mini." Cody pulled out her mini-tablet and saw an e-mail from Quinn, but when she opened it, it was totally blank.

She turned to Quinn, who was holding his own mini-tablet, and said, "There's nothing in this message!"

Quinn smiled. "It's invisible," he said mysteriously. "So no one can read it without knowing how to translate it." He shot a look over at Matt the Brat,

33

who'd been staring at the kids.

"So how *do* you read it?" Cody whispered so Matt wouldn't hear.

Quinn leaned in. "Select the message, then click 'Black' for the font color." He sat back.

Cody did as she was directed. Magically, words appeared on the screen: "I just wrote you an invisible note!"

"That is so cool!" she said, delighted to learn a new secret method of communicating. "How did you do that?"

Quinn held up his tablet. "Write your message, like normal. Then select it and change the font to white. Then send the message."

The kids spent the rest of the trip sending invisible messages back and forth.

As the scenery changed from tall city buildings and busy streets to wind-swept cypress trees and rolling sand dunes, she imagined what life must have been like two hundred years ago. There would have been no malls, no movie theaters, no parks or playgrounds—just the mission, surrounded by miles and miles of trees, bushes, rivers, and lakes.

Before she knew it, the bus pulled to a stop. Cody looked out the window and saw the mission on one side of the street and the campground on the other. She stepped out and surveyed the small city of tents, all empty and waiting for them to move in. Cool.

As she stepped out of the bus with her backpack, she glanced back at the mission. A man with a long beard, dressed in baggy clothes, and a woman with her hair tied in a scarf, also in baggy clothes, stood near the entrance. Cody wondered if they were tourists there to see the mission, too. But instead of heading inside, the couple turned and stared at the bus. *Weird.*

"Welcome to the Mission Trail Nature Preserve," Ms. Stad said as the sixth-grade students began gathering their backpacks. "Collect your things and drop them off at your assigned tents. Then we'll meet at the camp amphitheater in twenty minutes."

Cody and M.E. were excited to find they would be together. They found their tent, dragged their suitcases and sleeping bags inside, and unloaded their gear. When they were done, they met up with Quinn and Luke at the amphitheater, nestled under some trees.

"This place is awesome," Cody whispered to Luke, while Ms. Stad began reciting the history of the area. "It smells like pine trees. And our tent is so cozy."

Luke whispered back, "I know. I feel like I'm in the middle of the frontier. I can't wait till we start the hike."

Cody noticed Ms. Stad had grown quiet. She looked up to see her teacher staring at her. Busted! Cody made a zip-the-lip gesture and Ms. Stad nodded, then went on with her talk.

"You'll be following trail signs Mrs. Van Tassell and the other parent volunteers set out yesterday when they came to set up the camp. The signs will lead you to the mission museum. They're much like the ones used by trailblazers and Indians years ago. There will be three kinds of signs to watch for: stone signs, also known as stone talk. These are stones placed in special positions that indicate which direction to go. There are also twig signs, which are small branches that have been arranged in a specific way, and grass signs, which are handfuls of grass tied together—they also show where to go."

"What about smoke signals?" a kid named Spencer asked.

Ms. Stad smiled. "Good question, Spencer. The Plains Indians and Ojibwas did use smoke signals to communicate across long distances, but for us to use them now would be too dangerous, since they might cause an out-of-control fire. We're going to keep communicating simple and just use stones, twigs, and grass. Now, here's a special card with a list of symbols you'll find along the trail."

Ms. Stad and the other adults began handing out small cards printed with symbols and their meanings. Cody looked at hers and immediately started to memorize the codes.

After they all received their code cards, Ms. Stad called the kids to attention. "On the front are the stone, pebble, twig, and grass codes. On the back

Trail Signs	straight ahead	turn right	turn left	do not go this way
Stones				
Pebbles				
Twigs				
Long Grass				

you'll find more symbols: one that means 'danger' and one that means 'hidden message.' If you find a hidden message, write it down but don't disturb it for the next group. The team that figures out the answers to the hidden messages will get to make the first s'mores tonight at campfire."

A cheer went up from the students. Cody turned the card over and found the additional symbols and translations. Underneath were the numbers 1 through 4, with lines next to each number.

"How cool!" Cody said to the others. "This is perfect for us. It's all in code! And Luke's always going

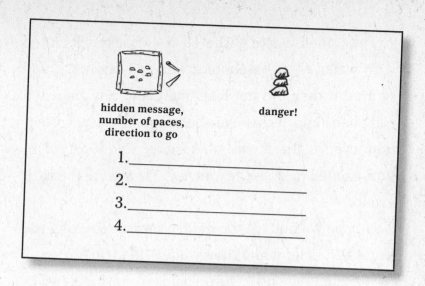

hidden message,
number of paces,
direction to go

danger!

1._____

2._____

3._____

4._____

on those orienteering trips. It should be easy for him."

Ms. Stad raised two fingers, the sign for "Quiet!" and everyone hushed. "You'll be going in groups of four, leaving every three minutes. The trail begins with a rock set on top of another rock, so keep an eye out for that first. Remember, stay with your buddies and do *not* leave the trail. There's a lot of poison oak around, so be careful. And we don't want you getting lost, so if you think you're in trouble, just call out for an adult. There will always be someone nearby."

The Code Busters gathered their backpacks filled with water, their notebooks, and cell phones. Cody figured if they did get lost, she could always use a cell phone app, like the air horn app, to attract attention, even if there was no service. The kids got in line, excited to start the journey. They were the fifth group.

"I hope we find all the hidden messages along the way," M.E. said while they waited their turn.

"I'm sure we will," Quinn said.

"I wonder what the messages will say," Luke said, picking up a long stick that lay on the ground nearby.

Cody said nothing, but she hoped that when they found the hidden messages they could crack the final code. After all, they were Code Busters. How would it look if they couldn't solve it!

Chapter 4

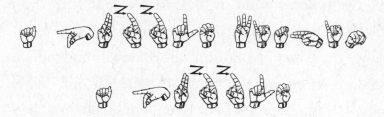

"There are the stacked rocks," Quinn called out when their group reached the starting point. He was pointing to two rocks, one on top of the other, a few feet in the distance. "The first trail marker! Let's go!"

The small group headed down the pine-needle-covered path, bordered on either side by pine and cypress trees. Cody heard birds cawing overhead and could smell the salty air of the ocean mixed with the woodsy scent. Finally! They were off on their adventure!

"Watch out for poison oak!" M.E. called, bringing up the rear of their single-file line. "I got it last year when my family went camping. I was covered in calamine lotion for a week."

Cody knew what to look for—a leaf with three arcs on each side, shiny, and either pink, red, yellow, or green. Although she'd never had poison oak, a friend back home had gotten it once when she fell into a creek bed. Even worse, she had broken both arms and had to wear casts over the poison oak! Cody couldn't think of a worse form of torture.

After hiking over the uneven terrain, the group soon came upon a split in the trail. Luckily, there was another trail marker—this one a V shape made from pebbles, with the tip pointing to the right. Cody thought how easy it would have been for someone—like Matt the Brat—to change the direction of the pebbles and get the Code Busters lost. Luckily, parent volunteers were posted along the route to make sure the kids were safe. Cody spotted one of the parents sitting on a bench a few feet ahead, holding a clipboard. Next to her was a miniature lighthouse made of wood and painted red and white. Cody marked the location on her map.

"Look! A hidden message!" Quinn called out.

Sure enough, Cody spotted a square made from twigs, lying on the ground ahead of them. Inside were six pebbles. Outside were two more twigs pointing to the right. Quinn stood at the edge of the message, facing the direction indicated by the V-shaped twigs. He walked six paces, his steps stiff and deliberate, and stopped by a hollow log that lay beneath a tree.

"You found it!" Luke said, catching up with Quinn.

Quinn bent over to reach into the log.

"Stop!" M.E. yelled. "There could be a snake in there!"

Quinn pulled his hand back.

M.E. was right, Cody thought. It was not a good

idea to go sticking your hand into a log when you couldn't see what was inside—even if the snake was not poisonous, and even if you had a snake kit, which they did. She knelt down and studied the log, then looked up at the tree branches above it. Hovering just over their heads, skewered on a branch, was a piece of green paper, nearly camouflaged by the leaves around it.

"There it is!" Cody said, rising.

Quinn stood up. The kids looked at the paper. It contained a drawing that resembled a bottle of soda pop.

Cody glanced at M.E. Quinn looked at Luke. They all frowned.

"What do you think it's supposed to mean?" M.E. said.

"A bottle of soda pop?" Luke added. "It makes no sense. Are we supposed to search for an actual bottle of soda? Are we supposed to drink some soda? I don't get it." He lifted his New Orleans Saints cap and scratched his head.

"I have no clue," said Cody. "Maybe we're supposed

to write down 'soda pop' and unscramble it, like an anagram.

M.E. jotted down the words and tried to rearrange them. She came up with:

sad poop (Everyone laughed.)

popas od (They laughed again because it sounded like, "papa was odd.")

sopadop (Which made no sense even if it was "soap a dope," but it was still funny.)

spodapo (Which made no sense at all and wasn't even funny.)

"Just write down 'soda pop' for now and we'll see what comes next. Maybe it will make more sense then," said Quinn.

Cody jotted down the clue in her notebook. The kids continued following the trail markers while keeping an eye out for other hidden messages. Cody knew there had to be at least three more, because there were four lines to be filled in on the card. They had to stay alert to the other signs, too, so they didn't miss any and go the wrong way. Cody recorded all the symbols they found on their route, and soon her notebook page was full.

Code Buster's Key and Solution found on pp. 167, 174.

Suddenly, Cody spotted another square with some pebbles inside and two twigs outside. "Guys, another message!" she announced.

Quinn, Luke, and M.E. gathered around the square.

"Eight pebbles inside this time," Quinn said, after counting them. "That means eight paces."

"The arrow is pointing that way," said Luke, gesturing to the left.

"Can I try to find the message this time?" M.E. asked. The others nodded and made way for her

46

to begin her paces. Her legs were shorter than the other kids', and Cody was a little concerned her steps might be off a pace when she finished. Taking that into account, Cody scanned the area where M.E. stopped.

"The message should be here somewhere," M.E. said, looking up at a tree that towered over her. The others glanced around, too, until finally Quinn said, "There! I see it—on that big rock! The message is written in chalk."

Sure enough, Cody saw the message that Quinn had indicated. This time it was a drawing of an animal.

"A duck?" M.E. asked, blinking her eyes.

"A goose?" Cody added, noting the longer neck.

"Maybe it's a swan," Quinn added.

"Or a turkey?" asked Luke, grinning.

Cody smiled at him. "I think you're the turkey," she said playfully.

"All right, so what do we have so far?" Quinn turned over the card. In the space underneath where he'd written "soda pop," he jotted down "duck-goose-swan?"

"Soda pop duck goose swan," Luke repeated. He said it again faster, then slower. Finally, he shrugged. "Dude, I got nothing. Figuring out the path is easy, but this part of the puzzle is hard. You guys solve it yet?"

The others shook their heads. Cody was finding this trail puzzle to be more difficult than she'd expected. She wondered how the other students were doing. As a Code Buster it wasn't getting the first s'mores that she really cared about—it was solving this puzzle!

"Let's keep going," Quinn said, noting the next trail marker. They waved to the parent volunteer as they passed by and continued along the path, being careful to follow the instructions and keep away from poison oak. Along the way they spotted a tower and marked it on the map. They'd been walking for nearly ten minutes, and Cody wondered how much farther they needed to go before arriving at the "building" shown on the map. She thought about getting out her cell phone and using Google Maps to look at the topography, but decided that was cheating. Besides, following the route markers was more fun. And they had at least two more clues to go.

Five minutes later Luke spotted another hidden-message symbol. This one led to a tree where they found a little rubber ducky hidden at the back.

"A rubber ducky?" M.E. said. "Seriously?"

"Well, it's definitely not a goose or a swan," Quinn said.

"Or a turkey," Luke added.

Cody picked up the rubber duck and turned it over. Written on the bottom in black marker were the letters "CK."

"Look," she said, "the two letters have a red circle around them, with a line drawn through."

"Ooookaaaay," Luke said. "So what does that mean?"

"Maybe it's a rebus," Cody said. She loved rebus puzzles, where pictures stood for words, like a pic-ture of a sheep—a ewe—meant "you." Sometimes the puzzles added or subtracted letters from the picture words. For example, if there was a picture of some meat, minus the letter *T*, that could mean "mea" or "me."

"You mean duck without the 'c-k'?" Quinn asked. "That would be du . . ."

"Or 'duh'!" said Luke, laughing.

"Well, it doesn't make much sense, but let's write it down," Quinn said. "Soda pop, duck, goose, swan, duck without the c-k, duh."

The puzzle was beginning to drive Cody crazy. Nothing she'd ever worked on was this hard. What was Ms. Stad trying to do? Not let anyone have s'mores?

They continued on their journey quietly, lost in thought. Cody went over all the clues in her mind but still couldn't come up with a solution. She checked the list with the four blank lines. They still needed one more part of the puzzle before they could really try to decipher it.

Just after she found a pond and marked it on the map, Luke spotted the next hidden-message symbol. It led to a nearby hole in the ground with a small sign stuck in the dirt. It read, "Who lives here?" with an arrow pointing to the hole.

Cody bit her lip, trying to come up with all the animals that lived in holes.

"It has to be some kind of burrowing animal," M.E. said.

"Duh," Quinn said. "There are about a million animals who live underground."

"Besides Bugs Bunny?" Luke asked, grinning.

Cody shook her head at his lame joke.

M.E. began listing burrowing animals: "Well, there are rabbits, chipmunks, moles, gophers, groundhogs . . ."

"Wait!" Cody said, noticing something on the other side of the sign. "There's a picture on the back." The Code Busters peered behind it and saw a drawing of a small slender animal. It was about a foot long, with reddish brown fur, a white belly, and a long tail.

"Oh," M.E. said. "That's a weasel."

Cody bet she was right. M.E. really knew her animals.

"You're sure?" Luke asked. "Looks like a rat to me."

"You can tell by the white belly," M.E. said. "And they burrow."

Cody sat down on a nearby rock and wrote down "weasel" on the last space on her card.

She read over the answers they'd filled in, then announced, "Guys! I know! I know the answer to the puzzle!"

Code Buster's Solution found on p. 174.

Chapter 5

"nother nursery rhyme?" Luke asked, rolling his eyes. "What are we, kindergartners?"

Cody laughed. But then, Luke always made her laugh. She thought he should be a stand-up comic when he grew up. But she knew he had other plans. With his strength and fearlessness, he would no doubt end up in some kind of professional sport—like Olympic skateboarding. Either that, or become a stuntman.

"Just write it down for now," Quinn said, busily jotting the title into his own Code Busters notebook. "I'm sure it will be important later."

The others did the same, then closed up their notebooks, stuffed them into their backpacks, and continued down the path. After a few more yards, M.E. spotted another one of the parent chaperones and alerted her friends.

"You made it!" Mrs. Vamvouris, Spencer's mom, said. "You reached the end of the trail! Good job! We're meeting over at the courtyard by the mission to wait for the others. You'll find snacks and drinks there." She pointed across the street, where other students who had completed the trek were gathered.

"Cool," M.E. said. "I'm starving. I hope they have something good."

As the four Code Busters headed for the courtyard, Cody looked at the historic mission. While she expected to see a small decaying building, worn by weather and time, the Carmel Mission seemed to be in perfect condition, and quite beautiful. She spotted a sign that read, MISSION SAN CARLOS BORROMÉO DEL RÍO

CARMELO—the official name of the mission. Another sign pointed to other buildings on the grounds, including the Junipero Serra School, the Basilica Church, and several museums.

The tall, round church inside the courtyard was the most eye-catching. The white adobe building featured two towers, a dome, and several crosses at the top of the highest peaks. To Cody, the mission didn't look as if it was more than two hundred years old! She couldn't wait to see inside.

The kids found a seat in the courtyard and enjoyed their boxed juices and trail mix. All except Quinn. He was too busy reciting the nursery rhyme under his breath and trying to figure out what it meant.

> *"All around the mulberry bush,*
> *The monkey chased the weasel;*
> *The monkey thought 'twas all in fun,*
> *Pop! goes the weasel."*

"That's not how it goes," M.E. said, when Quinn was finished. "I learned it like this."

"All around the cobbler's house,
The monkey chased the people.
The monkey stopped to pull up his sock,
Pop! goes the weasel."

"You're both right," Cody said, looking at her cell phone. "I did a search for the rhyme, and there are lots of versions. Here's another one."

"All around the chicken coop,
The possum chased the weasel.
The possum stopped to scratch his nose,
Pop! goes the weasel."

"Chicken coop? Possum? Never heard it that way before," Luke said.

"Here's another one," Cody said.

"Half a pound of tuppenny rice,
Half a pound of treacle.
Mix it up and make it nice,
Pop! goes the weasel."

"And another," she continued.

"A penny for a spool of thread,
A penny for a needle—
That's the way the money goes,
Pop! goes the weasel."

"How come there are so many versions?" Quinn asked, scrunching up his nose and looking confused. "How are we supposed to figure this puzzle out if one rhyme has a chicken coop and another one has treacle—whatever that is."

Cody didn't have time to look up the word *treacle*. Ms. Stad was waving two fingers in the air, trying to get the students' attention. Slowly, they stopped their conversations and settled down.

"Welcome to Mission San Carlos Borroméo del Río Carmelo," Ms. Stad said. "Congratulations on finishing the hike! Hopefully, you found the hidden clues and figured out the secret message."

Quinn raised his hand. "We figured it out, but we still don't understand it!"

Ms. Stad gave a knowing smile. "Just keep it in mind as you continue on your adventure. Now it's time for another piece of the puzzle. Our parent volunteers will hand you a paper with some pirate words and phrases. See if you can figure out what they mean before we begin our tour of the mission."

"Awesome," Quinn said as he took a sheet of paper from a parent. "I'll bet we get all of them."

Cody looked at her sheet. This was going to be fun! The first phrase was easy—she'd heard it a million times—but the puzzle got harder as she went on down the list.

1. **Ahoy there!**
2. **Avast ye!**
3. **Hornswoggle**
4. **Jolly Roger**
5. **Parley**
6. **Shiver me timbers!**
7. **Freebooter**
8. **Landlubber**
9. **Cackle Fruit**
10. **Davy Jones's Locker**

The Code Busters translated the ten phrases, then checked their answers with one another by tapping out Morse code so no one could understand them.

1. ···· ··   ▬ ···· · ·▬· ·

2. ··· ▬ ▬▬▬ ·▬▬·

3. ▬ ▬▬▬   ▬·▬· ···· · ·▬ ▬

4. ·▬▬· ·· ·▬· ·▬ ▬ ·   ··▬· ·▬·· ·▬ ▬▬·

5. ▬ ▬▬▬   ··· ·▬▬· · ·▬ ▬·▬

6. ·▬▬ ▬▬▬ ·▬▬

7. ·▬▬· ·· ·▬· ·▬ ▬ ·

8. ·▬▬· · ·▬· ··· ▬▬▬ ▬· ▬▬ ▬· ·▬·· ·▬ ▬· ▬··

9. ▬·▬· ···· ·· ▬·▬· ▬·▬ · ▬·   · ▬▬ · ▬▬· ···

10. ▬···· ▬▬▬ ▬ ▬ ▬▬▬ ▬▬   ▬▬▬ ··▬· ··· · ·▬

Code Buster's Key and Solution found on pp. 166, 174-175.

Luke recognized "hornswoggle" from a Bugs Bunny cartoon. Yosemite Sam often accused Bugs of hornswoggling him. Quinn and Luke both knew what a Jolly Roger was, but M.E. knew the literal translation, since she'd studied French as well as Spanish. "Jolly" was actually *jolie*, meaning "pretty," and "roger" was *rouge* for "red."

Next was "parley," and Cody knew this one from watching Johnny Depp as Captain Jack Sparrow, who used the word a lot. M.E. said "parley" was actually *parlez* in French.

"Shiver me timbers" was obvious—the exclamation point gave it away. They guessed at "freebooter" and "landlubber," thinking they had something to do with pirates.

"'Cackle fruit' is probably some kind of food," M.E. said, then made a guess and tapped it out in Morse code. The others agreed, even though it wasn't actually a fruit.

"'Davy Jones's Locker' was in a SpongeBob cartoon," Luke said. "Mr. Krabs ends up at the bottom of the sea in Davy Jones's Locker filled with smelly gym socks." He tapped out the meaning and the others compared their answers.

Just as they finished translating the pirate slang, Ms. Stad called everyone to attention.

"All right, students. If you've finished the puzzle, keep it handy. In a few minutes you'll find out the answers. But for now I want you to follow me. We're going into the basilica. Does anyone know what a basilica is?"

A girl named Mia from Cody's class raised her hand. "A church?"

"Correct! It's a church, so please be respectful. That means quiet. I'll lead you through it to the museum, where you'll meet a docent who knows all about the Carmel Mission and Pirate Hippolyte de Bouchard."

Cody heard murmurs at the mention of the pirate's name. The students gathered up their trash and tossed it in nearby cans, then lined up behind their teachers. Ms. Stad led the first group down the flower-lined courtyard, past the fountain, and through the wooden doors. Cold air and tall ceilings were the first things Cody noticed about the basilica. A student in the front of the line said, "Brrr!" and the word echoed throughout the cavernous chapel.

Someone began to play the organ, and the basilica filled with the song "Ave Maria." Cody thought it was the most beautiful sound she'd ever heard. As she passed by the pews, headed toward the front, she noticed there were only three people in the church. An elderly woman sat in one of the dark wood pews at the back, her bent head veiled, her hands clasped in prayer. Cody wondered what the lady thought about all these kids trooping through. On the other side stood a man and a woman who seemed out of place in their baggy clothes; they had sour looks on their faces. The man was dressed in a plaid shirt and old jeans and had a long gray beard. *Is that a toothpick in his mouth?* Cody wondered. The woman wore a large faded T-shirt and jeans, and had a long braid of salt-and-pepper hair down to her waist. Cody wasn't sure, but she thought they were the same two she'd seen when she'd gotten off the bus. As Cody walked by, she felt their eyes on her, and it creeped her out. She moved along quickly.

As she reached the altar, she noticed the soft light from the stained-glass windows made the chapel appear to glow, giving the intricate Spanish artwork an iridescent look. She wondered who had carved the figures and created the paintings. Missionaries? Indians? Professional artists? She looked down and saw a large rectangular slab in the stone floor, with a portrait at the far end. *In memory of Father Junipero Serra?* she wondered.

The students were led past a tiny room with discolored adobe walls, a stone floor, and a lone shuttered window. Inside sat a hard wooden bed, a wooden desk, a chair, and little else. Cody wondered if this was where one of the missionaries lived. How difficult it must have been for them, without all the comforts she and her friends had today.

Farther down the hallway they peered into another room, this one completely different from the one they'd just viewed. This room was twice the size and was filled with bookcases, chairs, a desk, artwork, and a fireplace. A simple candle chandelier hung from the wood-slatted ceiling. A colorful throw rug covered most of the tile floor. But Cody was most impressed by the number of books the shelves held. This had to be the mission's library. A quick look at the sign confirmed her guess.

Finally, they reached the main museum building. The room offered a glimpse into the past, with displays of rusty tools, tattered clothing, yellowed documents, broken beaded jewelry, and chipped cooking utensils. Cody found the jewelry especially interesting and wondered if the necklaces and brace-lets were valuable. They had to be, securely enclosed in their cases.

"Ahoy, mates!" came an accented voice from across the room. Cody turned to see an older man with a red beard and sailor's cap standing in an alcove at the back of the museum. She sidled up closer until she could see his freckled face clearly. He wore an antique-looking sailor's uniform to match his cap, reminding her of the pirates she'd read about in *Treasure Island.*

"He looks like Popeye," Matt the Brat said.

"I heard that!" the old sailor man said. "I don't likes me spinach!"

The students laughed at the funny interpretation of the cartoon character.

"Greetings, students from Berkeley Cooperative Middle School," he continued in his odd accent. Cody guessed he was either British or Australian, with a heavy dose of pirate on the side.

"Me name is Chad Bour—you can call me Chad. I'm an Aussie sailor from the land down under. This here uniform—we call it a naval rig, not a sailor suit—is a real imitation of an authentic replica of the ones made in the 1800s, and worn by all able rates and leading hands."

Cody enjoyed his funny way of talking. She studied the outfit, which resembled the modern sailor's dress uniform—all white with a blue collar, three stripes on the lapels, and, of course, bell-bottom pant legs.

Chad caught Cody staring at the hems of his pants. A pair of cowboy boots were sticking out from underneath.

"Like my bell-bottoms, do ye, lassie? We wear our hems wide so we can roll them up when we have to scrub the decks."

Cody wanted to ask about the boots, but figured she couldn't get a word in edgewise with this fast-talking character.

"And this here is a lanyard." Chad held up an

intricately tied cord that was looped around his neck. A key dangled from the end of it. "Lanyards were used to hold things, like matches to fire the cannons and knives for defense. I keep a key to the museum in mine so I won't lose it. Later on, you'll learn how to tie your own lanyards."

Cody grinned at the old sailor. He was off to a good start. He was fun to listen to.

Finally, Chad Bour began talking about the Carmel Mission Museum. The docent seemed to know a lot about the old adobe settlement, the five-foot-thick adobe brick walls, the artifacts on display, and the Ohlone and Esselen Indians who worked the mission. But it wasn't until he said the missionaries ate bear meat that she really tuned back in from her daydreaming about pirates.

"When Father Junipero Serra died in 1784, guess where they buried him."

Cody remembered seeing a small cemetery with graves lined with large seashells and raised her hand. "The cemetery?"

"You'd think so," Chad said, "but Father Serra was

special. You know the basilica that you all passed through? He's buried right beneath the chapel floor."

A few of the students gasped. Cody wondered why they buried the famous missionary there instead of in the cemetery, but she didn't have a chance to ask as Chad continued his story.

"The mission was in ruins after the pirate, Hippolyte de Bouchard, raided the place." He paused, glancing around at the wide-eyed group, then said, "Do ya want to hear the story of California's only known pirate?"

There was a chorus of "yeahs" from the crowd.

Chad Bour grinned, revealing crooked, yellowing teeth.

"Well, there was this Argentine pirate named Hippolyte de Bouchard who heard the California missions were filled with hidden gold, silver, and jewels. See this cross?" The docent picked up an ornate silver cross the size of a TV remote from the case and showed it to the kids. "They thought the missions were loaded with precious metals like this."

"Is that real silver?" M.E. asked. Cody's friend

loved to wear jewelry.

"This one was actually made of iron years ago by the blacksmith in the mission foundry, but he coated it with silver to make it shiny," Chad answered. "Anyway, Bouchard thought he'd gather a bunch of sea rats, load up his ship, and set sail for the Pacific Coast. While all the other pirates were pillaging the ocean off the East Coast, he had the West Coast seas all to himself."

Cody heard oohs and aahs from the students. They were eating this up—and so was she.

"When he attacked the Sonoma Mission and found nothing of real value," Chad continued, "he sailed on over to Monterey Bay. He was sure the missionaries there kept their treasures hidden. He'd heard talk of a secret vault located in the basilica that was said to hold rare jewels and priceless artifacts. But after pillaging, looting, and burning what he could, he and his two hundred men left the area empty-handed." Chad paused, grinned, and asked, "So do you think there really was a treasure?"

"Yeah," said Matt the Brat without raising his

hand. "But the pirates probably fought each other and couldn't find it. I'll bet I could find it."

Cody shook her head at Matt the Brat's bragging. He could hardly find his homework, let alone a hidden treasure. The missionaries had nothing to fear from him.

Chad nodded. "The missionaries did have a treasure, but they'd been forewarned about the pirates' planned invasion and hid everything."

"Where?" asked Luke.

"That's the question," Chad answered. "Unfortunately, the Carmel missionaries took the secret location to their graves. And no one has ever found the lost treasure, although many have tried."

"A lost treasure! Awesome!" Matt shouted without raising his hand. For that he got a sharp look from Ms. Stad.

A girl named Maddie raised her hand.

"Aye?" Chad said, calling on her.

"Do you think the treasure is still here somewhere?"

"To tell you the truth, missy, I do," Chad said.

"Years ago there was a treasure hunter—supposedly a descendant of Bouchard—first name, Franco. Rumor has it that he came close to finding it."

The students' eyes widened.

"But he mysteriously disappeared while searching for the buried loot. That was more than forty years ago. All they found was a knapsack with a journal containing cryptic notes and an old map of the mission and surrounding area. Oh, and a single piece of eight."

"Is that a gold doubloon?" another student asked.

"No, mate, the piece of eight is a Spanish dollar. It's made of silver, not gold."

Chad continued talking about the Spanish currency, even showing them a real silver coin from a black velvet pouch he had in his pocket, but Cody's mind was wandering. What had the old sailor said a few minutes earlier about a treasure hunter coming close to finding the treasure? What if the treasure wasn't buried, but hidden in some other way? Chad had just said that some of the mission's treasures, like the cross that was dipped in silver, weren't really all that valuable. If you can coat things in silver, maybe you can coat some treasures so they *don't* look so valuable.

Quinn turned to Cody and whispered in Pig Latin so no one could understand him: "Ee-way eed-nay oo-tay ee-say at-they ap-may!"

Code Buster's Solution found on p. 175.

Chapter 6

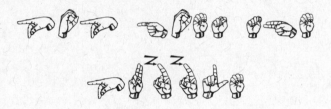

Chad continued with his presentation, distracting Cody from the treasure hunter's map and coded notebook. Luke took notes on Chad's explanation of nautical navigation, jotting down phrases like, "batten down the hatches," which meant prepare the ship for a storm, and "beat to quarters," which meant get ready for battle. Cody could just picture Luke on a pirate ship, climbing up to the crow's nest to look for other ships, or sword fighting on the plank like Peter Pan.

Quinn was fascinated by the sextant, a small instrument that looked like a complicated protractor with a spyglass attached. Chad told the students that sailors and pirates used sextants to plot the ship's course at sea by measuring the angle between two objects, like a star in the sky and the distant horizon. Cody had a feeling Quinn would get one the next time he went to the military surplus store. Then all he'd need was a ship.

Meanwhile, M.E. studied the map abbreviations that Chad had shown them. It was different from Ms. Stadelhofer's map and indicated how the sailors marked the waters. She'd already learned most of them, and was comparing his symbols with the ones on Ms. Stad's map. Cody was fascinated by how many different symbols and codes there were. The American Indians had their markers—tied grass. The trailblazers had theirs—arranged rocks. And the sailors even had symbols for the open seas . . . and for buried treasures. Cody found the orienteering symbols the most interesting. It seemed like everything on a map could be marked with a symbol—bridges, fences, towers, benches, ponds, pits, trees, bushes.

If they actually got a chance to see the treasure hunter's map, Cody hoped the Code Busters would be able to interpret some of the markings. Wouldn't it be awesome if the map actually led to a treasure? *Yeah, right . . .*

"Lunchtime!" Ms. Stad announced, after the students had had a chance to explore the museum. It was noon and Cody was hungry, in spite of the snack she'd had earlier. "Let's meet in the courtyard in five minutes," Ms. Stad said.

Quinn caught Cody's eye and began finger spelling.

Code Buster's Key and Solution found on pp. 169, 175.

Cody nodded, then pulled M.E. and Luke aside and finger-spelled the same message to them. While the other students slowly filed out of the museum, the four Code Busters lingered, pretending to be interested in some of the artifacts near the door. When the coast was clear, Quinn whispered, "I want to know more about that treasure hunter's map and notebook. Let's talk to Chad and see if he'll let us look at them."

Quinn approached Chad at the back of the museum as the old man gathered up the artifacts he'd shown to the students during his presentation.

"Excuse me," Quinn said.

Chad Bour looked up and gave a toothy grin to Quinn. "Aye, mate? Got a question for the old sea dog?"

M.E. giggled at Chad's unique way of talking. Cody wondered if the "old sea dog" ever really sailed the ocean. Maybe he was just an actor, playing a part to entertain the students who visited the mission.

Quinn nodded. "You know that treasure hunter you were talking about?"

"Bouchard!" Chad boomed, as if making an

important announcement. "Rumored to be a descendant of the pirate himself."

"Yeah, him," Quinn said. "Do you think we could see his map? And maybe his notebook?"

Chad squinted at the four of them for a long moment, and Cody wondered if there really was a map and notebook. Maybe it was all part of the act.

"Well, er, that's really part of my, er, the museum's private collection . . ."

Luke spoke up. "We're part of a club called the Code Busters, and we like to solve puzzles and crack codes. We just wanted to look at his stuff and see if we could figure out . . ." Luke paused.

"Figure out where the treasure be?" Chad said, finishing his sentence.

Luke nodded and smiled. "Yeah. We promise we'll be careful."

"Well, I like your enthusiasm. And I'm a code lover myself. I suppose that would be all right. But you'd have to be mighty careful. His things are very old and very valuable. Got it, mates?"

"Cool!" said Quinn. The other Code Busters

grinned excitedly. They were going to see something that the other students didn't get to see—a real treasure map. And a coded notebook.

"Wait here," the old man said. He headed for a door at the back of the museum with a sign that read STAFF ONLY.

"What about lunch?" M.E. whispered.

"Why are you whispering?" Quinn asked, frowning.

"I don't know," M.E. replied. "But Stad will miss us if we don't show up soon."

"She's right," Cody said. "Maybe one of us should go tell her we're checking something in the museum and we'll be right there."

"I'll do it," Luke volunteered, and headed out the door. As he left, Cody thought she spotted the baggy-clothed couple she'd seen twice earlier. This time they seemed to be watching the door.

Chad returned holding a stained, weathered knapsack and gently set it on one of the glass display cases.

"Whoa," Quinn said, admiring the leather bag.

The initial *B* was carved into the leather.

"Aye." Chad nodded. "Like I said, it's very old. And very valuable." He pulled apart the top of the bag that was held together with leather strings, reached in, and withdrew a rolled-up piece of paper, worn at the edges. Next, he pulled out a tattered notebook, bound in leather and tied closed with strings.

Quinn reached for the paper.

"Don't touch it!" Chad said sharply, his eyebrow raised.

Quinn withdrew his hand.

"I'll put it under glass so you can see it, but it'll still be protected." Chad untied the string around the map and gently unrolled it, then placed a sheet of glass on top of it. The Code Busters crowded around. *A real treasure map!* thought Cody.

"What's up?" Luke asked, coming up behind them.

"Check it out, dude!" Quinn said. He could hardly contain his excitement. Luke looked over Quinn's shoulder.

"Awesome!"

Quinn gazed up at Chad. "Can we copy it?"

"You mean, photocopy? No. Too delicate."

"No, I mean take a picture of it, with a cell phone?"

"I suppose that would be all right," Chad said.

Quinn turned to Cody. "You take the picture. I'll sketch it on a piece of paper and make it larger."

Cody focused her cell phone over the map and took a couple of pictures. Meanwhile, Quinn got out his Code Busters notebook, flipped to a blank page, and drew the map, adding all the marks and symbols.

"Hurry," Luke said to him. "We don't have much time until Stad comes after us."

Quinn nodded as he sketched the map.

"Could we see his notebook, too?" Cody asked, still holding her cell phone.

Chad smiled. "I think it's great when young people take an interest in this old stuff." He untied the leather string of the notebook and opened it to show the kids some of the entries. Turning the pages carefully, he explained what he knew about the contents. It was mostly the ramblings of Franco

Bouchard—descriptions of the area, details of the pirate Hippolyte de Bouchard, his own musings about chasing after the treasure.

When Chad turned to a page that looked different from the others, Cody raised her hand and said, "Stop!" She caught herself and blushed, then said, "Please."

Chad left the notebook open to the page Cody had indicated. The message that had caught her eye was printed differently from the other entries in the notebook. There were strange numbers underneath.

All I can find around this place is the path made of cobbler's stone. There's a bench that's carved with the form of a monkey that I have chased until I've tired. The only friend a weasel who thinks I'm the one acting the monkey, but my own thought is, that soon it will, I hope, all be worth it. In fact, though not fun, I shall see Pop when the man goes with me into the mouth of the weasel.

10-19-12-4-23-22-19-17   4-10
13-14-23-12-22-13

"Cody! MariaElena! You two boys! It's time to go!" Ms. Stad stood in the doorway, arms crossed, summoning them. Cody knew they had to leave.

"We're coming," she promised. She turned to Chad and quickly asked, "Do you mind if I take a picture of this part? It's really interesting."

"Be my guest," he said. "Just don't touch the notebook."

Cody snapped a couple of pictures, hoping the passage would be legible on such a small screen. As soon as they went to lunch, she'd copy down the page onto paper so they could see it more clearly.

"Now!" Ms. Stad commanded.

Cody turned to Chad. "Thank you so much," she said.

"Yeah, thanks," Quinn added, closing his notebook with a copy of the map.

"Let me know if you come up with something," Chad said.

Cody put her cell phone back in her backpack while Quinn returned his notebook to his. All four headed for the door where Ms. Stad stood waiting for them. Cody turned to give Chad a last wave of goodbye, but he was bent over the map, still propped open on the display case. She watched as he ran a finger over the glass . . . as if he were following a path.

Why, Cody wondered, *is he frowning?*

During the lunch hour, Cody copied the odd passage into her notebook. While the others ate their sandwiches, she read her reproduction aloud.

"It doesn't make any sense," M.E. said, after taking a bite of her cheese sandwich. Everyone had gotten the same bagged lunch. Cody wasn't a fan of cheese, but the school didn't allow peanut butter and jelly—her favorite—because too many kids had allergies. She'd traded M.E. her sandwich for her friend's apple.

"Yeah, just sounds like a bunch of jibberish," Luke added.

Cody read the first sentence out loud again. "'All

I can find around this place is the path made of cobbler's stone.'" She shrugged. "I don't know what that's supposed to mean. There are paths all over this place. And they're all made of stone."

Luke leaned over her shoulder and read the second sentence. "'There's a bench that's carved with the form of a monkey that I have chased until I've tired.' Kind of a funny way to talk," he said, "but maybe that's how they said things back in the day. Anyone seen a bench carved with a monkey?"

The others shook their heads. Cody continued the excerpt from the notebook: "'The only friend a weasel who thinks I'm the one acting the monkey.'" Cody paused. "Wait a minute! Listen to these words: 'monkey,' 'weasel,' 'cobbler' . . . Ring a bell?"

"It sounds like the nursery rhyme 'Pop Goes the Weasel,'" M.E. said.

Cody studied the page a few more seconds, then began circling more key words, including "chased," "fun," "Pop."

"Look! 'Pop,' 'goes,' 'the,' 'weasel'—there are three words in between each of those key words."

Working backward, she began circling every fourth word. She held up the paper for the others to see.

"You're right!" Quinn said. "All . . . around . . . the . . . cobbler's . . . bench . . . Every fourth word is part of the rhyme!"

Code Buster's Solution found on p. 175.

Luke lifted his baseball cap and scratched his head. "So you think this treasure hunter wrote down a coded nursery rhyme? But that still doesn't make any sense."

Cody's shoulders sagged. Luke was right. What did "Pop Goes the Weasel" have to do with treasure?

"Let's ask Chad when we go back in after lunch," M.E. said, wrapping up the crusts of her second sandwich. She never ate crusts. She'd heard they made hair curly, and she thought her hair was curly enough.

Ms. Stad called the students to attention once again. "All right, everyone. I want you to stay with your buddy and follow me. Our docents have a few activities planned for you in the museum before we head back to camp. As Chad mentioned, the mission was mostly self-sufficient, and they made almost everything themselves. Now you're going to learn how to make hardtack bread, drip candles, knotted lanyards, and writing utensils. We'll divide you into small groups so you'll all get a chance to do everything. Everyone ready?"

Cody loved crafts and was glad she got to do the lanyard activity first. The students filed back into the museum and headed for their assigned stations. Four docents, including Chad, stood in four different areas, waiting to share their crafty knowledge. Cody and M.E. gathered with several other kids at a table filled with bowls of colorful twine. A docent name Cheri Eplin showed the group how to knot the twine into a kind of necklace, and soon Cody and M.E. each had a lanyard to wear around her neck. Cody planned to keep her pen in her lanyard.

At the next table, they learned how to make hardtack, a kind of cracker/bread made from flour, water, and salt, and baked four times to make it hard and long-lasting on sea voyages. But it wasn't easy to eat, and many of the sailors called the bread "molar breakers" because they'd crack their teeth on it. The docent, Brian Ostrewski, encouraged the kids to try a small bite, but Cody thought it tasted like a rock, and decided the hardtack might be better to throw at critters who tried to enter her tent at night. She didn't have plans to ever make hardtack again.

Candle making turned out to be the most fun. Tammy Gaylord, the docent manning the table, showed them how to dip string into melted wax—over and over again—to make a multilayered, multicolored candle. After the candles cooled, the students would get to take them home.

Cody was glad to find Chad at the final table, teaching students how to make their own writing utensils and invisible ink. "Do you kids know how to make invisible ink like the pirates did?"

Cody raised her hand. "I wrote a secret message with a white crayon on white paper and it looked invisible. But when you colored over the paper with another crayon, the words would appear."

"Aye, that's a great idea. But the pirates didn't have crayons, so they used lemon juice. After they wrote a message, the person who received it held it over a lantern, and the words magically appeared. That's what we're going to do today."

The students were given pointed sticks made from a tree branch and then asked to write a short note on a piece of paper using lemon juice in small bowls.

"Let's write ours in reverse alphabet code," Cody suggested to M.E.

The girls pulled out their notebooks and turned to the page with the reverse alphabet code. In the first line, the letters were in order—*A* to *Z*—from left to right. Underneath that line, the letters were written in the opposite direction, from *Z* to *A*.

Cody and M.E. began writing their secret, coded messages, matching the first letter of the first word on the top line with the letter directly underneath on the bottom line. Since the first letter of Cody's message was *T*, she found the letter *T* on the first line and wrote down the letter that was underneath—*G*—using the invisible ink.

G-S-R-H   R-H   H-L   U-F-M!

When Cody finished, she traded messages with M.E., blew on the message until it was dry, then held it over a lightbulb. Both girls squealed in delight as the invisible words became visible. Cody quickly translated M.E.'s message:

R D-Z-M-G G-L Y-V Z K-R-I-Z-G-V!

Code Buster's Key and Solution found on pp. 171, 175.

When the activities were over, Ms. Stad let the students visit the museum store to buy souvenirs. But once again, the Code Busters hung back to talk to Chad as he cleaned up the secret-message supplies.

"Mr. Bour?" Quinn said.

"Aye, call me Chad. Oh, it's you guys. Did you make anything out of that map or the message?"

"Well," Quinn said, "we figured out the message. It's that nursery rhyme, 'Pop Goes the Weasel.' Every fourth word is part of the rhyme. We just can't figure out why he wrote it."

Chad nodded. "Ah, mates, you see, back in the days of yore, pirates often sent coded messages in rhyme. There were lots of things they didn't want anyone to know about, as you can imagine."

"That's what Ms. Stad said about the nursery rhyme we read in class." Cody looked at the others.

"So there's another meaning?" M.E. asked Chad.

"That there be," Chad said, with a twinkle in his eye. "I'll give you a hint, but the rest is up to you."

The Code Busters nodded, eager to get a clue to the message.

"I'll tell you this—the word 'monkey' isn't about a monkey at all."

"What's it mean?" Luke leaned in, frowning.

"It means 'cannon,'" Chad said simply.

"Cannon?" Quinn repeated.

"Can't you tell us more?" M.E. pleaded.

Cody noticed the gleam in Chad's eye suddenly disappear. His face darkened, and his deep frown returned. He was staring at something behind the kids. Thinking it might be Ms. Stad, Cody whirled around, ready with an excuse for why they were hanging back.

But in the doorway stood the man with a long gray beard and a woman with a long salt-and-pepper braid down to her waist. Both were thin, had dark, piercing eyes, and wore baggy shirts and jeans.

Cody immediately recognized them from the basilica. The sour expressions hadn't left their faces.

"Howdy, Chad!" the man said, around the tooth-pick hanging out of his mouth.

Chad stomped around the table in his cowboy boots toward the pair.

"Get out of here, you slimy bilge rats, before I call the cops!"

Chapter 7

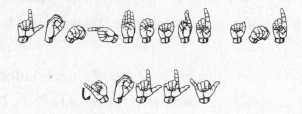

I mean it, Longbeard, you bilge rat. Get out! And take your old sea hag, Jolly, with you. Or I'll—"

"Or you'll what, Bour?" the man called Longbeard asked. "Keel haul me? Make me walk the plank? Ha! I see you're still filling these youngsters' heads with yer fish tales about hidden treasure." The scraggly old man turned to the kids. Even from a few feet away, Cody could smell his foul breath when he spoke to them. "Don't believe a word this landlubber spews, kiddies. He's been lying about a so-called hidden treasure for decades. Just telling tall tales—that's what he does best."

"You got that right," the woman named Jolly added. She was staring at Chad in a peculiar manner, one eyebrow raised, a smirk on her face.

"Get out, the pair of you!" Chad shouted. He grabbed an antique sword from the wall and held it high.

The hairs on the back of Cody's neck stood up. *What is going on between these three? Is Chad really a liar? Why is he so angry at the old couple? Will he really use that sword?*

"Ha!" Longbeard laughed. "I'd like to see you try." He spat his toothpick on the floor, then grabbed Jolly's bony arm and pulled her back.

"You haven't seen the last of me, Bour," he called. Then he and the woman retreated outside.

Chad slammed the door shut on the couple. Cody saw the sword in his hand shaking. The kids were too terrified to move—M.E. appeared frozen to her spot—but Cody figured they'd better get out of there. She glanced around, wondering how they would escape the museum with Chad blocking the door.

And holding a sword in his hand.

To her surprise, Chad turned around and faced the kids, grinning like a happy dolphin.

"All part of the act!" Chad said as he returned the sword to its place on the wall. "Just rehearsing one of our upcoming scenes. Hope we didn't really scare you."

Cody let out a breath. She saw M.E. visibly relax.

Luke forced a laugh. "Cool," he said, but to Cody, he didn't sound or look as if he meant it.

"Yeah," Quinn repeated solemnly. "Cool."

Cody and M.E. were too stunned to say anything.

"Were they actors?" Quinn asked.

"Not real actors," Chad said. "Old friends of mine. We used to go treasure hunting together, years ago. Just a hobby. Nothing serious. Never found much of anything."

Hmmm, thought Cody. *If they aren't actors, they sure did a good job. But they don't seem like old friends.* Before she could ask a question about the odd couple, the door swung open again. Cody spun around, expecting Longbeard and Jolly to be standing in the doorway armed with their own swords—or worse.

But it was just Ms. Stadelhofer.

"Oh, you're still here," Ms. Stad said to the Code Busters. She turned to the students who were lined up behind her. "All right, class. Come in quietly. Mr. Bour is about to give you the answers to the pirate puzzle, so get your papers out and be ready."

Chad Bour was back to his old friendly self as he welcomed the students into the museum and explained the meanings behind the pirate expressions. When he was done translating, Chad continued with his presentation by holding up a black flag that featured a skull and crossbones in the center.

"The flag is called a Jolly Roger," he said. "It comes from the French term *jolie rouge*, which means 'happy red.' But this ain't a happy flag, not with a skull and crossbones on it. That symbolizes death. Pirates used the symbol to frighten other ships, thinking it would make them easier to conquer. Even the colors of the flag are codes. Black means death, white means surrender, and red means 'show no mercy.' Flags have been used to communicate between ships for centuries."

Cody and her club members already knew semaphore code, where each letter of the alphabet was represented by the positions of two flags. The first letter of her real name—Dakota—was made by holding one flag straight up and one straight down. Sometimes the Code Busters just used their arms to communicate in semaphore code, when they didn't have any flags.

Cody turned to the other Code Busters and spelled out four letters using the semaphore code.

Code Buster's Key and Solution found on pp. 168, 176.

"So you already know semaphore, eh?" Chad called out to Cody. She blushed. "Well, here are three flags you might want to learn, in case you're ever in danger," Chad said. He held up the first flag, yellow with a blue horizontal stripe in the middle. "This means 'watch out!'" He held up a second flag, a red triangle on top of a yellow triangle. "This means 'man overboard!' And this one—white with a red X—means 'help!'"

Cody jotted down the flags and their meanings in her Code Buster notebook, thinking they might need them someday if they were ever in real danger at sea. She thought it would be fun to make the flags at their next club meeting.

"That concludes your tour this afternoon, students from Berkeley Cooperative Middle School," Chad said. The crowd gave him an enthusiastic round of applause.

He bowed in thanks. "You're all welcome to peruse the rest of the museum. Pleasant voyage!" With that he disappeared behind the door in the back, where Cody had seen him retrieve Franco Bouchard's knapsack, map, and journal.

The kids shuffled off, free to investigate the museum. After fifteen minutes, Ms. Stad collected all the students in the main room. Suddenly, the lights went out, plunging the windowless room into darkness. Cody froze. M.E. grabbed her arm and held it tight.

"What happened?" someone whispered. Cody heard students repeat the question.

Just then, an ear-piercing foghorn sounded at the back of the room.

Then came the loud boom of a cannon being fired.

Several students screamed. M.E. tightened her grasp on Cody's arm.

"Calm down, everyone," Ms. Stad whispered to the group. "It's all in fun."

Cody turned in the direction of the noise and saw a strange glow, like lighted fog. The eerie cloud filled the back of the room. A ghostly image rose up from the fog, unfurling a red-lined white cape with dramatic flair.

There stood a pale-faced pirate, dressed all in white except for the inside of the cape.

The ghost pirate laughed, a booming hollow laugh that sounded as if it came from an echo chamber.

And then the ghost spoke: "Beware the spirit of

Hippolyte de Bouchard, who haunts the mission in search of a long-lost treasure . . ."

The spooky fog faded away, along with the pirate.

The museum lights flickered back on.

"That was awesome!" Jody said.

"What was that?" M.E. asked.

"Did you see his face?" a student named Maile questioned.

Cody smiled. She knew the ghostly pirate had been Chad. She'd recognized his cowboy boots under the white bell-bottom pant legs. She wished docents on other field trips were as entertaining and exciting as he was.

Under Ms. Stad's direction, the students began filing out of the room to prepare for the trek back to camp. Just outside, Cody spotted the pair she'd seen earlier at the museum lurking nearby. They leaned against the building, eyeing the kids. *Creepy*, Cody thought.

"Lima, Oscar, Oscar, Kilo," Cody said to the other Code Busters as they gathered in groups outside. She was using the phonetic alphabet code to talk with her friends, so eavesdroppers—such as Long-beard and Jolly—wouldn't understand what she was saying.

After receiving Cody's message, Quinn, Luke, and M.E. glanced around to see what she was refer-ring to.

"Whisker, Hotel, Echo, Romeo, Echo?" Quinn asked.

Cody nodded in the direction of the couple.

"Tango, Hotel, Echo, Mike!" M.E. said, recogniz-ing the pair.

"Sierra, Uniform, Papa?" Luke asked.

Code Buster's Key and Solution found on pp. 167, 176.

Cody shrugged. That's what *she* wanted to know. Why were these two still hanging around? Some-thing was going on. She only wished she knew what it was.

"All right, students," called Ms. Stad. "It's time to make your way back to camp. You'll be following a new map. As you travel along, you're to write down each trail marker you see. For example, if you see this marker"—she held up a sign that showed two parallel lines—"that means 'bridge.' If you find a bridge along your way, draw it on the map using the symbol for bridge that's on the bottom left corner of your map. You get points for each of the symbols you find, so use your eagle eyes."

"What do we win?" Matt the Brat called out.

"Nothing. It's just for fun," Ms. Stad announced.

Matt pumped his fist into the air and yelled "Yes!" before he realized there was no prize.

After waiting in line for their group to proceed down the path, the Code Busters began the trek back to camp. All four of them had a great time searching for items on the map. By the time they reached the end of the trail, they'd found them all.

"That was awesome!" M.E. said after they'd turned in their completed maps. The students spent the next half hour washing up and preparing for their campfire dinner of hot dogs, veggies, s'mores, and apple cider. After the meal, they gathered around the campfire for stories and songs, led by Luke and Quinn's teacher, Mr. Pike.

First he led them in a round of "Silver and Gold":

"Make new friends, but keep the old, one is silver and the other's gold."

"Now we're going to sing some sailor shanties," said Mr. Pike. "Does anyone know what a shanty is?"

"An old house?" offered a student named Lillian.

"It can be, but in this case, it means 'to sing.' It comes from the French word *chanter*."

Cody wondered why so many words came from French. She remembered Ms. Stad telling the class that a lot of coded messages originated in France, like the one the French resistance used during World War II. They had code names, symbols, poetry, and even coded articles in newspapers. Using numbers to represent page numbers, lines, and words, people communicated without the enemy intercepting their messages.

"Sailors and pirates used to sing while working on their ships," Mr. Pike continued, interrupting Cody's wandering thoughts. "It helped keep the men together and lifted their spirits during long voyages at sea."

Matt the Brat shouted, "Yeah, SpongeBob sings shanties on his show!

Mr. Pike nodded patiently, then continued. "A lot of shanties have double meanings that only the sailors and pirates understood. I'm going to teach you one tonight called 'Blow the Man Down.' Ready?

"Oh, blow the man down, bullies, blow the man down!
"*To me way-aye, blow the man down.*
"Oh, blow the man down, bullies, blow him right down!
"*Give me some time to blow the man down!*

"Do you know what this particular shanty is about?" asked the teacher.

Luke raised his hand. "The wind blew the pirates down?"

"Actually," Mr. Pike said, "it refers to all the heavy work the pirates had to do aboard ship. The phrase 'blow the man down' really means 'give me strength to do the work.' Who knows the song 'Fifteen Men on a Dead Man's Chest'?"

Most of the hands went up.

Mr. Pike continued, "If you've read *Treasure Island* by Robert Louis Stevenson, you might already know that Dead Man's Chest is actually a small island in the Caribbean Sea. The story goes that Blackbeard the Pirate left fifteen of his men on the island to punish them for breaking the Pirate Code of Conduct. The worst thing a pirate could do was mutiny, which means to rebel against the captain or to leave the ship without permission. If he did, he could be marooned."

Quinn raised his hand. "That happened in *Pirates of the Caribbean*. Captain Jack Sparrow was marooned after his men mutinied."

Cody heard a couple of students say, "I loved that movie!"

"What's the Pirate Code of Conduct?" asked a student named Thomas.

"Believe it or not, pirates did have rules," said Mr. Pike. "Many of them covered things like how to share the loot and how the crew was paid. They even had a rule for turning out the lights and candles by eight o'clock. Every pirate had to sign a contract—or mark it with an X if he couldn't read or write. And most of them couldn't do either."

Unable to read or write? Cody thought. *How did they get along in life without being able to do that?*

"We have to check out that Pirate Code of Conduct. It sounds awesome," Quinn whispered to the others.

"I doubt it's anything like our Code Buster rules," M.E. said, grinning.

"Shall we sing 'Blow the Man Down' again?" Mr. Pike asked.

Once they'd sung the shanty three more times, the teacher announced, "Well, it's eight thirty. According to the Pirates Code of Conduct, it's past time for lights out."

Cody heard groans from the other students, but she was tired from the day and ready to curl up in her sleeping bag. The girls took showers in the cinder-block latrine, dressed in their pajamas, and brushed their teeth—all while watching out for spiders.

Once they were snuggled in their sleeping bags, Cody found she couldn't get to sleep. Maybe it was all those pirate stories that kept her awake. Or maybe it was the mystery of that strange couple arguing with Chad. Then again, maybe she was just excited about the possibility of a treasure hidden somewhere at the mission.

Rolling over on her stomach, she propped herself up on her elbows and peered out the mesh door of the small tent. Most of the other tents were dark, except for a few flashlights moving around inside.

Suddenly, Cody saw a flash of eerie light, coming from somewhere in the dark woods that surrounded the campsite.

The light began to flash on and off.

Cody began to recognize letters.

Code Buster's Key and Solution found on pp. 166, 176.

Someone was sending a message in Morse code . . .

Chapter 8

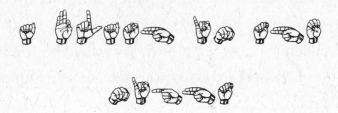

M.E.!" Cody whispered urgently, shaking her sleeping friend's arm.

"Huh?" M.E. mumbled, then rubbed her eyes and sat up. "What's wrong?"

"Look! Outside the mosquito flap! I saw something . . ."

M.E.'s eyes widened, and she scrambled forward. "What is it? A bear? A wolf—"

"No!" Cody said, cutting her off before she scared

both of them with her wild guesses. "Lights. Flashing on and off. I think someone is sending a Morse code message. Something about finding a map!"

M.E. peered through the mesh for a few seconds. "I don't see anything. But I'm never going to be able to sleep tonight."

"Keep watching! Over there." Cody pointed in the direction where she'd seen the flashing light.

"It was probably just one of the teachers or parents, checking on the—" M.E. gasped. "I saw it! You're right. It does look like Morse code. Someone's out there!"

"Write this down," Cody commanded, handing M.E. her notebook and a pencil.

Code Buster's Key and Solution found on pp. 166, 176.

Once the girls had translated the message, they looked at each other.

"What does it mean?" M.E. asked Cody.

Cody shrugged. "You don't suppose one of the boys sent that message . . . ?"

"Luke or Quinn? But why? That makes no sense," M.E. said.

Just then Cody heard her cell phone chirp. "A text." She picked up the phone lying next to her sleeping bag and read the message.

"*R U sending code?*" The text was from Quinn.

"*No,*" Cody texted back. "*Thot U wr.*"

After a pause, she texted again: "*Sup?*"

"*IDK. Something abt a map,*" Quinn answered.

Cody thought about the map Chad had shown them. She pulled up the picture she'd snapped on her cell phone and studied it. Was this the map they were referring to? She opened the tent flap and leaned out, scanning the dark again for the flashing light.

There was nothing but pitch blackness in the trees around the camp. Whoever had been sending Morse code appeared to have vanished.

Another text chirped on Cody's phone, again from Quinn. "*We'll CIO 2morrow. L8R.*"

Code Buster's Solution found on p. 176.

M.E. snuggled back into her sleeping bag and pulled it up to her nose. Although she'd been frightened, it didn't take her long to fall back asleep. Meanwhile, Cody kept watch for the next half hour, unable to relax. Finally feeling drowsy—and seeing no sign of the mysterious light again—she lay down in her bag and drifted off, dreaming of pirates.

The warm sun filtering in through the door of the tent woke Cody early the next morning. She turned to check on M.E. and found her friend still asleep. Cody checked her phone for messages and, finding none, gathered her clothes, towel, soap, and toothbrush, and headed for the latrine to get ready for the day.

By the time she returned, M.E. was up and dressed and holding Cody's phone. "Quinn just texted. He said to meet him in the trees where we saw the light last night."

Wondering what was up, Cody tucked her Pj's into her sleeping bag, hung up her wet towel on a tree branch, and, together with M.E., headed for the spot where they'd seen the flashing light. Luke and

Quinn were already there, scoping out the area.

"Did you find something?" Cody asked as she and M.E. reached the boys.

"Footprints," Luke said, pointing to what looked like several large boot prints in the soft dirt.

"They look fresh, but I guess they could have been made any time in the past few days," Quinn said.

"There's no sign of a flashlight or map, is there?" M.E. asked, scouring the area around the footprints.

"Yeah, right," Luke said. "Like they'd leave those behind."

"I wonder if it was one of the teachers?" M.E. said. "Maybe Stad was practicing Morse code with another teacher so she could send us a message today. She loves codes about as much as we do."

"I doubt it," Quinn said. "Not that many kids would be able to translate it."

Something caught Cody's eye as she followed the boot prints leading deeper into the trees. The object was small, thin, and white, and sticking out of the ground. If she hadn't been looking carefully, she might have missed it.

She knelt down for a closer look.

"Come here!" she called to the others. "I think I found something."

"What is it?" M.E. asked, hurrying to Cody's side. The gang knelt down around the object in the dirt, frowning at the discovery.

Cody reached for it.

"Don't touch!" Quinn commanded.

"Why not?" Cody asked.

"Because it probably has germs." Quinn grabbed the bottom of his T-shirt and used it to grasp the tip of the sharp object. He held it up.

A toothpick.

The kids looked at one another.

Then Quinn said aloud what they were all thinking: "Longbeard was here."

Luke nodded. "He was chewing on a toothpick when we saw him. Remember, he spat one out at the museum."

"Gross," M.E. said, making a face.

Cody shivered, creeped out by the thought that the angry old man who'd been hassling Chad was the one hiding in the dark trees while she and her friends slept. What was he doing out here? Who was he signaling to?

The camp bell rang, calling the kids to breakfast. The Code Busters returned to Quinn's tent to drop off the puzzling toothpick, but as they were about to leave, Cody saw Quinn staring at his backpack.

"What's the matter?" Cody asked.

"My backpack. It was on the bed, and now it's on the floor." Quinn began rummaging through the pack. After pulling out all of his stuff, he sat back, frowning. "The map I copied . . . you know, the one the treasure hunter made?"

"Yeah?"

"It's gone!"

"Boys and girls," Ms. Stad called after the students had finished their buckwheat pancakes, bacon, and strawberries. "Gather 'round, please."

Over breakfast the Code Busters had discussed the missing map. Who had gotten into Quinn's backpack? Longbeard and Jolly? How had they gotten in without being seen? Was that the map they'd referred to in Morse code? And why would they want to steal it?

"It's time for another day at the mission," Ms.

Stad continued, interrupting Cody's thoughts. The students mumbled under their breath, excited about more map puzzles. Cody hoped they'd see Chad so she could ask him about Longbeard and Jolly. Maybe he knew why the old couple might want the map.

Each student was handed another of Ms. Stad's maps for a return trip to the mission. This time they were given a list of objects to find when they reached the mission itself.

M.E. smiled. "This should be easy."

1. ✕ ✕ ✕ _____

2. ◯ _____

3. ⋀ _____

4. _____

5. ⌐†¬ _____

6. 🚩 _____

Code Buster's Key and Solution found on pp. 166, 176.

"Let's search the area fast," Quinn said, eager to find each of the objects in the puzzle. The Code Busters headed for the flower garden and jotted down the location on their maps, using the codes they'd been taught. Next, they headed for the courtyard fountain and marked it on the map. Finding all nine bells took some time, but Cody had kept an eye out for them earlier, since Ms. Stad had told them they'd be searching for the bells. They found the last one in the courtyard on top of a circular cement pedestal. Cody noticed this bell appeared to be cracked.

One of the docents had told the students that the bells were made out of bronze because they produced a nicer sound. But if the mixture of softer metals—tin, copper, lead—wasn't accurate, the bell could crack.

Cody leaned in and ran her finger along the crack, wondering why the mission employees didn't fix it. She thought she saw a glint of something bright deep within the crack. Could that be tin or copper?

"Come on, Cody," Quinn said, interrupting her thoughts. "We still have a few more to find."

Cody nodded, and they set off in search of the stone wall. By the time they were finished with the search, they realized they were the first ones to complete the challenge.

Quinn looked at his military-style watch.

"We've got some time before the rest of the kids are done. Cody, let me see the picture you took of the treasure hunter's map."

Cody got out her phone, tapped the picture, and handed it to Quinn. The map filled the small screen. Enlarging it with his fingers, he pointed to a section of the map. "What's that?"

"Enlarge it again," Luke said.

"Looks like a drawing of a big rock," Quinn said. They took turns studying it up close.

"Yeah? What's so special about that?" Luke asked.

"Why would a big rock be noted on the map?" Quinn asked.

Before anyone could answer, Cody said, "Guys, look over there." She pointed to the cemetery several yards away, where they'd found their last clue.

"I don't see anything except a couple of gardeners."

"Those aren't gardeners," Cody said. "Look at that beard!"

Finally, the others saw what she had: Longbeard and Jolly standing near a big rock. Each held a shovel.

"What are they doing?" M.E. asked.

"It looks like they're planning to dig in the cemetery," Cody said. "I'm pretty sure they shouldn't be doing that."

"Maybe that's why they're acting like gardeners. Did you see their matching shirts?" Luke said.

"Do you think they're digging up old bones?" M.E. asked, watching them from behind a large bush.

"I'll bet it's the treasure they're after, not bones," Quinn said. "That's probably why they stole our map. Come on. Let's go get a closer look."

The Code Busters headed for some nearby bushes, keeping out of sight of the two treasure hunters. When they reached their hiding place, Quinn turned around and finger-spelled: .

After a few minutes, they inched closer to the cemetery. Cody held her breath and stepped carefully, not wanting to make a noise. Quinn stopped a few yards away from the couple, behind another large bush, and finger-spelled: 👆👍👌👌👍🤙.

Code Buster's Key and Solution found on pp. 169, 176.

Hidden behind the hedge, the kids stood still, straining to hear what the two suspicious characters were talking about.

"It has to be here!" Longbeard said to Jolly, swinging the shovel around the area that surrounded the large rock.

"We've been all over this place!" Jolly snapped back. "We can't go digging up everything in broad daylight. We'll be arrested."

"We're not digging up the ground. We're planting flowers, remember?" Longbeard nodded toward a half-dozen marigolds in little cartons. "That's why we're wearing these stupid shirts and using that stupid sign on our van."

Cody took a closer look at the shirts. She could see the lettering more clearly now: GREEN THUMB GARDNERS.

Wait a minute. It didn't say "gardeners." It said

"gardners!" They'd probably made their own shirts and had misspelled the word!

She was about to finger-spell to the Code Busters when she heard a crack from behind her. She turned to see M.E. biting her lip and looking down at a twig she'd just stepped on.

The kids ducked and froze. Cody didn't dare breathe as she peered through the leafy wall of the shrubbery.

Longbeard's and Jolly's heads shot up. They listened for a few seconds, not moving.

"What was that?" Jolly asked Longbeard.

The grizzled old man shrugged. "Probably some animal creeping around."

"Or one of them kids," Jolly said, scanning the area. "There's too many of them here."

Longbeard laughed. "That's just it. They're the perfect distraction. No one's going to notice us with all them rug rats running all over the place. Now start digging."

"Maybe we better go check on our 'guest' first," Jolly said, glancing toward a parking lot a few yards beyond the cemetery.

Longbeard threw his shovel down. "Jeepers, you're such a worrywart! Go on and check if you have to, but hurry back. We don't have much time. And try not to attract too much attention, will ya?"

Cody and her friends remained still and watched Jolly head for a small panel truck parked in the otherwise empty lot. A sign on the van read GREEN THUMB GARDNERS, with the same misspelled word.

Quinn turned to Cody and signed:

Code Buster's Key and Solution found on pp. 169, 176.

Cody nodded, then she took Luke's hand and pulled him behind the bushes. Together they tiptoed toward the lot, staying close to the plants for camouflage. Cody saw Jolly reach the van and pat her pockets, then frown. The old woman knelt down and felt under the passenger wheel well. Seconds later she rose, holding a key in her hand. Looking around as if to make sure the coast was clear, she yanked open the side door.

Cody couldn't make out what was inside—it was too dark. But whatever it was made a moaning sound, like the cry of a wounded animal, just before Jolly slammed the door shut and relocked it.

Something—or someone—was locked up inside that van.

Chapter 9

Cody and Luke looked at each other, eyes wide, both holding their breath. Who—or what—was in that van? They had to find out, but if they were caught now, who knew what would happen to them? They might end up inside the van, too.

And then what?

They watched as Jolly relocked the door, then bent over and rehid the key under the wheel well of the van. But instead of straightening up as

Cody expected, Jolly got down on her knees and retrieved something from the ground. She stood up, stared at what looked like a sheet of paper, then wadded it into a ball and tossed it into a nearby bush. With a last glance around, she headed back to the courtyard where she'd left Longbeard digging.

Cody and Luke waited until Jolly was out of sight before coming out from their hiding place.

"What should we do?" Luke asked.

"We have to find out what's in there!" Cody whispered. "Whatever it is, it doesn't sound happy."

"Maybe it's a sick or hurt animal," Luke said. "If it's hurt, it could be dangerous."

"What about that piece of paper Jolly found and threw in the bushes?" Cody asked.

"Think it has anything to do with what's inside?" Luke said.

Cody shrugged. "There's one way to find out." She headed over to the large leafy bush where Jolly had tossed her trash. Maybe the paper was nothing, but maybe it was a clue. Cody reached in and pulled out the wadded ball. Uncrumpling it, she frowned as she walked back to Luke.

"Look at this," she said, showing him the wrinkled paper.

Code Buster's Solution found on p. 176.

Luke glanced at it. "There's nothing written on it—just two red streaks."

"White with red diagonal lines. Doesn't that remind you of one of those flags Chad showed us?" Cody suggested.

Luke studied it. "Yeah . . . but I forget what it means."

"It means 'help!'" Cody said. "And it might have come from inside the van." Cody held the paper up to her nose. "It smells like blood! Come on. We have to find out what's going on!"

Luke nodded and led the way to the van. When they reached the vehicle, Cody bent down and located the hidden key while Luke kept watch. She stood up and handed it to Luke.

"Keep an eye out," Luke said, taking the key.

Cody nodded. She kept her eyes focused in the direction of the cemetery, where Jolly and Long-beard were working. She only hoped Quinn and M.E. were staying out of sight. One more crack of a twig underfoot and they might be goners.

Luke jammed the key in the lock.

Cody glanced at him. "Be careful! It could be anything in there."

Luke nodded. "Just keep watching out for those two crooks. And give me your cell phone."

Cody frowned, puzzled by his request, but she dug in her pocket, pulled out her phone, and handed it over. Luke touched the flashlight app and held it up toward the door. Slowly, he pulled back the sliding door and shined the light inside.

A large figure was curled up in a ball, its back to the door.

It moaned again, as if it was in pain.

Luke focused the light on the figure as he opened the door wider.

Cody peered over his shoulder.

"What is it?" she whispered, ready to run at a moment's notice if it was a wild animal.

"It's not an animal," Luke said.

Another groan.

Cody gasped as the figure rolled over.

A man lay there, his hands and feet bound.

In spite of the blood on his forehead and the handkerchief tied around his mouth, the face was instantly recognizable.

Chad Bour.

"What happened to you?" Cody asked, as Luke handed her back her phone, then reached in and untied the gag. He began working on the knots that held Chad's hands and feet.

Chad panted, trying to catch his breath. "Those

scoundrels . . . they stole me map . . ." He sounded drowsy, his words coming in tired bursts.

Cody had seen people acting like this on her mom's favorite TV show, *CSI*. She hoped Chad would be okay.

"You mean the treasure hunter's map? The one you showed us?" Luke asked, freeing Chad's legs. Then Luke began on the rope tied around Chad's wrists.

"Yeah, they've been after it for years . . . knew I was on to something . . . They overheard me talking to you kids at the museum and thought I told you where the treasure was." He blinked several times, then rubbed his wrists where the rope had been.

It had to have been Longbeard and Jolly who stole the map from Quinn's stuff! Cody thought. "He sneaked into our camp and took the map Quinn drew!"

"Luckily, Quinn wrote everything we figured out in code," Luke said. "I doubt they could crack it."

Cody nodded as the puzzle pieces came together. "So they got you to give them Captain Bouchard's actual map, then kidnapped you and stowed you in their van!"

"Yep. Hit me over the head." Chad touched the back of his head and winced. "Then tied me up."

Although Chad still seemed groggy, he was starting to sound more like himself.

"We've got to get Chad out of this van and to a doctor," Cody said to Luke. "I'll call 911." She punched in the numbers.

While she made the call, telling the dispatcher where they were and that they'd need an ambulance, Luke pulled Chad forward by the legs until the old man could touch the ground with his feet. Then he eased Chad out of the van, and helped him stand, supporting him with his shoulder.

"Cody, help me take him over to behind those trees, and we'll hide him there until the cops come, in case those two come back."

Cody glanced in the direction of the courtyard. Luckily, the coast was still clear.

The two kids wrapped their arms around the old man, helping to support him. Chad was thin and light, and they were able to walk him several yards away to a safe hiding place.

After they had gently laid him on the ground behind the shady trees, Luke turned to Cody. "Go find M.E. and Quinn, and tell them to get out of there. They could be in danger. I'll stay here with Chad until the cops come."

Cody nodded and started toward the graveyard, then heard tapping coming from behind her. Recognizing the familiar pattern, she paused and listened.

-.-. .- .-. . ..-. ..- .-..

Code Buster's Key and Solution found on pp. 166, 177.

Luke was tapping Morse code to warn her. She smiled at his concern, then continued walking, staying close to the bushes as she passed the van. But before she got much farther, she heard a voice and ducked down out of sight.

"Knew I heard something!" Cody heard Jolly saying.

"Now we gotta get rid of them, too," Longbeard growled angrily. "So where are those other two?

Must be around here somewhere."

Cody heard M.E.'s muffled cries as the couple held on to the kids and dragged them roughly toward the van.

"We'll lock them inside with Bour until we can finish digging," Longbeard said. "Then we'll get rid of all of them. For good."

Cody had to think fast. As soon as Longbeard and Jolly reached the van and discovered Chad was gone, who knew what they might do to Quinn and M.E.? She quickly came up with a plan that she hoped would distract the two creeps long enough to give the cops time to arrive. Ducking behind a row of shrubbery, Cody made her way back to the spot where the couple had been digging.

As soon as she reached the mound of dirt, she heard a loud curse coming from the parking lot.

Longbeard and Jolly had reached the van. And apparently, they hadn't liked what they saw—an open door and a missing Chad Bour.

There was no time to lose. Cody screamed at the

top of her voice: "I found it! I found it! I found the treasure!" She was sure that would bring Longbeard and Jolly back to the cemetery.

She crossed her fingers, hoping that her plan worked. If she could just stall them long enough for the police to arrive . . . Otherwise, she could end up trapped in that van with her friends.

And then what?

Seconds later, Jolly and Longbeard came running toward her.

Cody stood frozen to the spot, feeling panic well up inside her.

Her two friends weren't with the old couple.

What had happened to Quinn and M.E.?

Longbeard and Jolly rushed to her. "Where is it?" Jolly demanded. "Show me, you little punk! Now! Or you'll be joining your friends for a long ride off a short pier."

Cody strained to listen for a police siren but heard nothing. "The secret to the location is in here," she said, pulling her notebook from her backpack. She opened it to the page she'd copied from the treasure hunter's journal. There was the coded nursery rhyme that the Code Busters had deciphered. Trembling, her heart beating in hyper-speed, Cody held up the page. "This . . . this is it!" she said.

Longbeard snatched the notebook out of her hands. "This? It's nothing but a bunch of scribblings. Where's the treasure?"

"That's just it. This is a code that leads to the treasure. If you use it with the map, you'll find the spot."

Longbeard frowned. "Show me!"

Cody pointed to every fourth word as she recited "Pop Goes the Weasel." When she finished, she looked up at the grizzled old man. "Get it?"

Longbeard shook his head. "It's baby talk! Stop stalling! Where's the treasure? Or I'll lock you up with the others."

She thought of M.E. and Quinn locked in the van and kept talking, making up her story as she went along. Remembering what Ms. Stad had said about nursery rhymes having double meanings, she decided to give this one her own interpretation.

"Well, the first line of the rhyme, 'All around

the mulberry bush,' means that we have to look for a mulberry bush." Cody scanned the area, then pointed to some berry bushes that lined the edge of the cemetery. She had no idea what kind they were, but betting these two weren't really gardeners, she figured they wouldn't know, either.

"'The monkey chased the weasel' obviously means that the pirates chased someone—probably the missionaries—when they attacked the mission looking for treasure."

She looked up at a frowning Longbeard, who seemed to be losing patience. Quickly, she continued.

"And then it goes, 'The monkey thought 'twas all in fun.' That means that the pirate was enjoying himself . . ."

"And 'Pop! goes the weasel'?" Jolly asked, tightening her grip on Cody's arm. "What's that supposed to mean?"

"It's obvious," Cody lied. "Weasels like to burrow, so it popped something in the ground." Cody was quite pleased with her storytelling skills, and she wondered what Ms. Stad would think of her interpretation.

"So where's the treasure?" Longbeard demanded again.

"Show us! Now!" Jolly jerked Cody's arm.

"I'm trying to tell you. It's under the mulberry bush."

Longbeard glanced around the area. "But which one? There's dozens of them!"

Cody thought fast. "Oh . . . uh . . . see these numbers at the bottom of the page? Those are coordinates. All you need is a compass—"

"A compass! We don't have time to find a compass!"

"I have one," Cody said. "If you let go of my arm, I'll get it out of my pocket."

Jolly eyed her suspiciously. "I'll get it." She dug into the pocket of Cody's hoodie and pulled out her cell phone.

"There's no compass in there. Just your phone," she said. "You think we're stupid? I ain't giving you this phone so you can call the cops."

"No, no, there's a compass app on the phone," Cody said.

"What's an app?" Longbeard asked.

Cody had a feeling that these two old treasure hunters were not tech savvy. "Look," she said, trying to take the phone from Jolly.

"No way," Jolly said. "Tell me what to do. And do it fast!"

"Okay, just slide the bar on the screen over with your finger and touch that little square with the circle and lightning bolt. That's the compass app."

Jolly frowned at the unfamiliar gizmo. "It don't look like a compass," she said, but she released her grip on Cody and followed her directions. After a few failed attempts, she managed to slide the bar over and find the app.

"Good! Now touch the square," Cody said, encouraging the woman.

"This one?" she said, pointing to the icon Cody had described.

"Yep, just tap it and the compass will appear. Then you can enter the coordinates and find the right bush."

Jolly looked at Longbeard; he nodded his agreement.

Cody held her breath, hoping her plan worked. Otherwise . . .

With a last menacing look at Cody, Jolly tapped the app.

A loud siren filled the air.

Chapter 10

Cody's trick had worked! When Jolly touched the app icon on Cody's cell phone, the place filled with the ear-piercing sound of a police siren.

"You just hit the 'Panic' button and called the police!" she shouted to the surprised couple.

Longbeard and Jolly froze, eyes darting around in search of the cops. Jolly dropped the phone.

"Come on!" Longbeard said. "We gotta get outta here!"

Longbeard took off in the direction of the van. Jolly ran after him.

Cody picked up the phone and quickly followed, hoping the siren would attract the attention of anyone around who could help. By the time she reached the van, after Longbeard and Jolly, the cops had arrived. Quinn and M.E. were being helped out of the van by one of the uniformed officers. Dry tears streaked M.E.'s face. Two other officers were putting Longbeard and Jolly in handcuffs.

"Good," Cody said breathlessly when she saw her friends were safe. Luke appeared moments later from behind the trees where he'd hidden Chad. Cody noticed his arm was covered in blood and cried, "Luke! What happened?"

Luke looked down at the mostly dried blood and tried to rub it off. "Oh, I'm fine. It's Chad's blood. Must have got some on me while I was untying him."

"Where's Chad?" Cody asked, anxiously glancing toward the spot where they'd hidden him.

Just then, a couple of EMTs appeared from the trees, pushing a gurney. Chad was lying on his back, bandaged, with an oxygen mask over his face. Cody and Luke ran to his side as he was wheeled toward the waiting ambulance.

"Mr. Bour! Are you okay?" Cody asked, looking down at his bandaged head with concern.

Chad pulled the oxygen mask down. "Ay, thanks to you kids, I'm gonna be okay."

He started to replace the mask, then said in a gravelly voice, "Did you figure out the puzzle?"

M.E. and Quinn, who had joined them, shook their heads, along with Cody and Luke.

"Come by the hospital later, and I'll tell you how to decipher it," he said, then replaced the mask and closed his eyes.

"Is he going to be all right?" M.E. asked one of the EMTs.

"He'll be fine," the woman said. "He's got a pretty bad gash on his head, but he'll be all right. You can see him this afternoon."

Cody turned around to ask the police officer nearby a question and noticed a large crowd had gathered. Ms. Stad and Mr. Pike were standing behind a yellow police line, eyebrows raised, mouths open. The other students were buzzing on the sidelines, no doubt trying to figure out why the police were there, who the two people in handcuffs were, and what was wrong with the docent guy on the gurney. Not to mention why their four classmates were involved.

"Hey, Cody!" Matt the Brat yelled from the sidelines. "You're in deep doo-doo this time!"

Ms. Stad shot him a glance that stopped Matt from saying anything else. She warned her class to stay put, then ducked under the police line and headed for the Code Busters.

"What on earth is going on?" she asked when she reached them. "Are you all right?"

The officer who had freed Quinn and M.E. spoke for them. "They're fine, thanks to their quick action. And so is Mr. Bour. If it weren't for these kids, he might have been in real trouble."

Ms. Stad bit her lip. Silently she gave each of the four kids a hug. "What exactly happened?" she asked again.

Quinn shrugged. "We were just looking for the treasure that Mr. Bour had talked about."

"He had this treasure hunter's map and a journal page that were clues," Luke added. "We thought maybe the Code Busters could figure it out."

"But I thought that was all legend," Ms. Stad said. "Mr. Bour was just trying to make history come alive for you students."

"Yeah," Luke agreed, "but when we talked to him after the presentation, he said there really had been a treasure hunter: a descendant of Hippolyte de Bouchard who might have found the treasure. He's the one who left behind the map and puzzle that Chad had."

"What puzzle?" Ms. Stad asked. "What are you talking about?"

Cody became distracted as she watched the officers place Longbeard and Jolly in the back of one of the police cars. She wondered what would happen to them.

M.E. answered Ms. Stad's question. "We found a message that had a nursery rhyme hidden inside."

"'Pop Goes the Weasel,'" Quinn offered. "Only we couldn't figure out what the rhyme *actually* meant. We were going to ask you, Ms. Stad, since you know so much about hidden messages in nursery rhymes."

Ms. Stad smiled proudly. "Well, let's see. I do know that it's a rhyme about pirates who were searching for loot that was supposedly hidden inside 'the monkey.'

"Oh, remember what Chad said. 'Monkey' means 'cannon,'" Quinn said.

Unfortunately, there aren't any cannons at the Carmel Mission. There used to be, but they were melted down and formed into bells."

Ms. Stad looked at the disappointed faces of the Code Busters. She patted Cody and M.E.'s backs, smiled at Luke and Quinn, and said, "But it was still fun doing the treasure hunts and orienteering codes and other puzzles, right?"

The kids nodded, but their hearts weren't in it. They'd hoped to find treasure, and they'd found only dead ends, unanswered questions, and bad guys.

"Students!" Ms. Stad hollered back to the crowd

of kids watching the scene. "Time to head back to camp." She turned to the police officer. "Are these kids free to go?"

"I have a couple more questions; then you can have them back," the officer said.

"All right, I'll have one of my parent volunteers wait for them in the courtyard and make sure they return to camp safely. Thanks, Officer."

"Thank you, ma'am. You've got some smart kids here, you know."

"Oh, I know, Officer," Ms. Stad said, smiling at the group. "I definitely know."

The officer took down the statements of each Code Buster, one at a time. Since Cody had been the first one questioned, she sat on a bench to wait for the others and think about the puzzle. Pulling out her notebook, she flipped open to the page where she'd copied Bouchard's journal entry. Together the Code Busters had solved the odd message when they realized "Pop Goes the Weasel" was hidden inside. But there had to be more to it . . .

Quinn joined her on the bench.

"What are you doing?" he asked.

"I think there's something more here."

"But Stad said the rhyme meant the treasure was hidden inside a cannon—and there are no cannons around here."

"I know, but look at these numbers at the bottom," Cody said, pointing to the row of random numbers.

"Yeah, so? We figured they were some kind of numeric code, remember? But we couldn't decode them without the key. That's how codes work, dude."

Cody rolled her eyes at Quinn. "I *know* that. But that's just it."

"What's just it?" Luke said, appearing next to them. "What are you guys working on?"

"Cody thinks there's more to the puzzle," said Quinn, "and that these numbers have something to do with it:

10-19-12-4-23-22-19-17   4-10   13-14-23-12-22-13

But unless we have the decoder, we're not going to be able to figure it out."

"I think we have the decoder," Cody announced. "I think it's right here on the page."

Luke looked down at the message. "Where?"

"Remember how French words are sometimes used by pirates?" Cody said.

"Yeah," Luke answered. "You think it's French?"

"No, but remember what we learned about how the French resistance used to code their messages?"

"You mean, by counting pages, lines, and words—or letters—to encode them," Quinn said.

"Well, what if Bouchard's descendant, the treasure hunter, did that, using these numbers? And instead of using page numbers, lines, and words, he just used letters?"

M.E. came bouncing toward her friends, a grin on her face. "I'm done. That was fun. Anyway, I guess we should get back to—" M.E. glanced down at the nursery rhyme page Cody held in her lap and stopped midsentence. "Hey, what's up?" She sat down on the bench next to Quinn.

"Cody's trying to figure out what the numbers mean," Quinn said, nodding toward the journal entry. She began writing numbers in order, under each of the letters in the first row of the rhyme. Then she located the numbers written at the bottom of the journal entry and wrote down the corresponding letter.

All around the mulberry bush
1 2 3   4 5 6 7 8 9   10 11 12   13 14 15 16 17 18 19 20   21 22 23 24

The monkey chased the weasel
1 2 3   4 5 6 7 8 9   10 11 12 13 14 15   16 17 18   19 20 21 22 23 24

The monkey thought twas all in fun
1 2 3 4 5 6 7 8 9 10 11 12 13 14 15 16   17 18 19 20   21 22 23 24 25   26 27 28

Pop goes the weasel
1 2 3   4 5 6 7   8 9 10   11 12 13 14 15 16

Checking the number 10, she wrote down the corresponding letter, which was *T*. The next number was 19, which equaled *R*. She continued to write down letters for numbers in the code until she recognized a word.

She tried the set of letters in the next row, but the letters didn't form a familiar word.

After she tried the next two rows, she was about to give up when she decided to return to the top row.

145

This time it worked—they had the second word!

"Just one more word!" Cody said excitedly. Using the same top row, she decoded the last few numbers.

"Whoa!" she said to the others, who were grinning at the message. "Now we really *have* to talk to Chad!"

Code Buster's Key and Solution found on pp. 171, 177.

Chapter 11

M s. Stadelhofer is awesome," M.E. said, as the kids entered Community Hospital in Monterey, accompanied by Mrs. Van Tassell, one of the parent volunteers. Ms. Stad had called the Code Busters' parents to tell them what had happened. Then, the police had gotten the Code Busters special permission to visit Chad, as a reward for their "heroic efforts."

"I know!" Cody said. "It was so nice of her to let us

visit Chad while the other kids went back to camp. I hope he's okay."

"You don't have long, guys," Mrs. Van Tassell said. "Remember, he's recovering from that attack and will need lots of rest. Five minutes."

Cody was excited to see the docent and make sure he was all right. Not only had the police arranged for the kids to visit him, but an officer had stopped by the camp to inform the Code Busters they'd be getting a commendation from the mayor.

He also told them that Longbeard and Jolly were being held in the county jail on charges of kidnapping, illegal trespassing, theft, and several other counts. After a brief search of the thieves' trailer, the police found a large cache of valuable artifacts stolen from several museums in the area. They recovered most of the loot, except what the thieves had sold at local flea markets. Cody wondered if Chad knew all this.

Two hours later the kids entered the dimly lit hospital room and found Chad lying on his back in the bed, his head and wrists bandaged, his eyes closed.

He was connected to an IV and an electronic monitor beeped as it kept track of his heart rate.

He opened his eyes, and a smile lit up his face when he recognized the four kids. "Crikey!" he said in a gravelly voice. He coughed, cleared his throat, and said, "It's the code-busting treasure hunters who saved my life. Many thanks to ye."

Cody grinned, pleased to see how well Chad looked, in spite of everything. Aside from the bandages, he seemed to be his old self.

"How do you feel?" Quinn asked, gazing in awe at all the medical equipment in the room.

"Better than a barnacle on a bunion," he said.

Cody had no idea what that meant, but she figured it was good.

"Did you hear about Longbeard and Jolly?" Luke asked.

Chad nodded. "I expect they'll spend the rest of their lives in prison. Luckily, the cops found most of the treasure they stole."

"Yeah, they said a lot of it came from the mission museum," M.E. said.

"Ay, I've had my eye on them for some time," Chad said. "I noticed things went missing right after they visited the place. I didn't have any proof, but I banned them from returning. Still, they kept trying to sneak in and help themselves to more loot. That's why I chased them out of the museum during your tour."

"Why did they kidnap you?" Cody asked.

"They heard me talking about the treasure with you kids," Chad explained. "They knew you had a copy of the map, so they went looking at your camp. When they found the drawing in your stuff, they stole it. But you guys wrote all the clues in code." Chad grinned. "Pretty clever," he added.

Quinn's eyes lit up. "I knew it! I knew they stole the map out of my stuff. We saw them snooping around the camp area—well, we didn't actually *see* them, but we saw someone flashing Morse code and we found a toothpick and some footprints. I knew it had to be one of them."

Chad took a breath, coughed, and adjusted himself on the bed.

"Are you all right?" Cody asked, worried that the old man might have more serious injuries than they thought.

"Fine, just a bit stiff from being tied up in that van."

Cody was relieved that Chad would be fine.

"So you still haven't told us how you got kidnapped," Luke said.

"Or about the treasure," Quinn added.

"I'm getting to that," Chad said, a twinkle in his eye.

Cody smiled. At least his storytelling skills hadn't been affected.

"When those scallywags found out they couldn't read your map, they wanted the original," Chad continued. "They came back to the museum and made me hand over the real map. I thought they'd leave me alone, but they conked me over the head and took me with them. Tied me up and threw me in that van of theirs. Thank goodness you found me. Otherwise, I'd have been . . ." He drew his finger across his throat.

Cody shuddered at the thought. Maybe it was true. If they hadn't come in time, Chad might not be here right now.

"Yikes!" M.E. said, speaking for all of them.

"Kids, it's time to go," Mrs. Van Tassell said. "Mr. Bour needs his rest so he can get back to being a wonderful docent at the museum."

The kids nodded and began to shuffle out. But before they reached the door, Chad said, "Wait a minute. One more thing. Did you figure out the solution to the journal entry?"

The kids turned back to Chad.

"We found the nursery rhyme—'Pop Goes the Weasel,'" Cody replied. "Our teacher told us 'monkey' meant 'cannon' and that's where the pirates hid the money. But we never saw any cannons at the mission."

"And we finally figured out what the numbers at the bottom meant," Quinn continued. "Each one represented a letter in the first line of the rhyme. The message turned out to be 'treasure at museum.' Do you think the treasure is actually hidden somewhere in the museum?"

"Oh yes," Chad said, "but not the kind you're thinking of. There's no silver pieces of eight or gold bars. The real treasure is in the two-hundred-year-old artifacts that were found at the mission. In total, they're worth hundreds of thousands of dollars. That's why Longbeard and Jolly were so eager to rob the place."

Quinn held up a hand. "Hey, was there ever a *real* Bouchard ancestor?" he asked Chad. "Or was that just another one of your stories?"

"Oh, he was real, all right," Chad said. "And he found plenty of treasure—all in the form of valuable artifacts that he donated to the museum."

"Then what happened to him?" M.E. asked. "Did he get rich?"

"No. But after donating his finds to the mission, he got rich in other ways."

"How?" M.E. asked.

"After fifty-some years of treasure hunting, he retired and went to work as a docent at the museum, where he could see his treasures every day while sharing them with others," Chad said.

153

"Just like you?" M.E. asked.

Cody caught something in Chad's eye—a glint of mischief? Was he telling another one of his wild stories? And then she gasped. "You're part of the puzzle! That's your map and your journal!"

Chad's toothy smile widened.

The other Code Busters looked at her, frowning. "What are you talking about?" asked Quinn.

"Don't you get it?" she said. "'Chad Bour' . . . the letters are an anagram!"

Luke got out a pencil and wrote down the name on a sheet of his notebook paper. He happened to be a master at unscrambling letters and words.

"Bouchard!" Luke exclaimed.

The kids stared at Chad Bour—aka Bouchard.

"Are you really a descendant of the pirate Hippolyte de Bouchard?" M.E. asked.

Before Chad could answer, a nurse appeared in the doorway. Mrs. Van Tassell nodded at her and said, "Time to let Mr. Bour rest."

"Wait, one more second," Chad/Bouchard said. "I have something for your Code Busters Club." He reached over to the table near his bed and picked up a small velvet sack that lay there.

"Where did you get that?" Cody asked.

"Tucked it into my sock so those two wouldn't find it," he answered. Pulling apart the strings at the top, he opened it, stuck in two fingers, and withdrew something shiny.

"I want you kids to have this, to thank you for all you've done. You truly saved a 'man overboard,' and I'll be forever grateful."

He handed the silver coin to Cody. She knew immediately what it was—a real piece of eight! From a real treasure hunter!

"Cool!" she said, holding it up for the others to see.

Chad handed her the velvet bag. As Cody started to replace the coin inside, she felt something touch her fingers. She pulled out a piece of paper that was rolled up like a tiny treasure map. She unrolled the paper and read the words from a familiar camp song, using the mirror app on her cell phone:

Make new friends,
But keep the old.

One is silver,
And the other gold.

Code Buster's Solution found on p. 177.

Cody smiled at Chad, then rolled up the paper and inserted it back inside the bag along with the coin. The Code Busters thanked the old man and reluctantly waved good-bye. Cody wondered if she'd ever see Chad Bour again.

As they walked back to Mrs. Van Tassell's car, Cody held the velvet bag tightly in her hand. She knew exactly what the Code Busters would do with it. Keep it, hide it, and create a map to its secret location so only *they* would be able to find it.

Suddenly, a thought came to her.

"Mrs. Van Tassell!" she cried. "Can we stop by the mission one more time before we go back to camp? I think I know where the real treasure is!"

Quinn, Luke, and M.E. looked at Cody as if she'd lost her mind.

"What are you talking about?" Quinn asked. "Chad told us where the treasure is—in the museum. It's the artifacts."

"That's where he *thinks* it is," Cody argued. "But I think we've all missed something."

"Like what?" Luke asked.

"Well, if I'm right, I'll show you," she said. "Please, Mrs. Van Tassell? It's really important. And it'll only take a few minutes, I promise."

Mrs. Van Tassell checked her watch. "All right, but make it quick. Your teacher was nice to let you go to the hospital, and you don't want to take advantage of that."

Cody sat back in her seat, fingers nervously fidgeting with the velvet bag that held the silver coin. The clue had been there all along. While the kids hadn't found any cannons on the mission property, there had been cannons when Bouchard searched the mission.

Most of the early cannons were made of bronze—and Ms. Stad said the mission's cannons had been melted down and turned into bells. The large bell in the middle of the mission plaza—the one with the crack—was bronze. Cody remembered noticing something shiny inside the crack. At the time, she figured it was just a play of the light. Now she thought otherwise.

Maybe it was silver.

Chapter 12

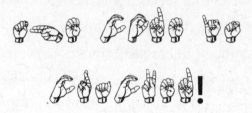!

M rs. Van Tassell drove into the mission parking lot. Cody quickly got out of the car, followed by the other Code Busters and Mrs. Van Tassell.

"Come on!" she cried. She made a beeline for the center of the mission, where the cracked bell had been placed among a bed of flowers. She ran up to it and peered closely at the crack, hoping she hadn't just imagined what she'd seen. Pulling out her phone, she tapped the flashlight app and shined it into the crack.

Definitely shiny!

"Do you see?" Cody asked, standing back so the others could get a look.

"I see a crack," M.E. said.

"Look closely," Cody commanded.

Quinn stared at the jagged line on the bell. "Wait a minute, M.E.! Can I have one of your barrettes?"

M.E. looked at him strangely but removed the metal barrette from her long brown hair and handed it to Quinn.

Quinn held it by the edge and began scraping the inside of the crack. Bits of dirt crumbled down.

Are those bits of bronze coating? Cody wondered.

"What are you doing, Quinn?" Luke asked.

"Children!" Mrs. Van Tassell said breathlessly when she finally caught up with them. "I don't think you should be doing that—" She stopped, gasped, and covered her mouth with her hand. "Oh, goodness! Is that what I think it is?"

"Silver!" M.E. squealed. "The bell is made out of

silver! We're going to be rich!"

The others laughed.

"This isn't 'finders keepers,' M.E.," Cody said. "It belongs to the Carmel Mission. Come on, we've got to tell someone. I just wish Chad was here to see this. He's going to be so excited when he hears."

The kids, accompanied by Mrs. Van Tassell, headed for the museum to report their find. At first they were met with disbelief by the staff, then shock, then excitement. Cody insisted they call Chad at the hospital and report the news.

"Mr. Bour," Cody said on the phone, "we found the treasure you've been looking for."

"What do you mean?" Chad said, sounding sleepy. Cody was sorry to wake him, but thought he'd definitely want to hear the news.

"One of the mission bells is actually made out of silver. It was hidden underneath of coat of bronze. Remember what we learned about how the missionaries melted down all their silver? They must have reshaped it into a bell and covered it in bronze to camouflage it. It looks just like the other bells that were made from old cannons—except for the crack. That's what gave it away."

"Of course!" Chad said, now sounding awake and alert. "Silver is a soft metal, so it was bound to crack over time. You've found the treasure I've been looking for all these years! I don't know what to say! I'm so glad I met such expert treasure hunters and smart code busters!"

Cody hung up the phone, pleased that she and her friends had found the real treasure when so many other treasure hunters couldn't. *Sometimes*, she thought, *whatever you're searching for is right in front of your nose.*

"How did you figure it out, Cody?" M.E. asked as they headed back to Mrs. Van Tassell's car.

"The silver coin that Chad gave us is what got me thinking," Cody said. "It reminded me of the shiny crack in the bell, which I thought was weird at the time. A crack should be dark inside, not shiny. Then I remembered Ms. Stad talking about the cannons being melted down and turned into bells. That's what the other bells are made of. But that one was made of silver, then covered in bronze to disguise it."

"Just like that cross Chad showed us, remember?" Luke added. "He said it was made out of iron at the mission foundry by blacksmiths, like all their tools and cannons, but it was coated in silver to make it fancier."

"Exactly!" Cody said. "Only this time, it was the opposite. Silver was coated in bronze to make it plain, so no one would suspect how valuable it was."

"Cool," Quinn said. "Hiding silver under bronze is sort of like creating a code. It's something hidden within something else!"

"And we 'cracked' the code!" M.E. said. "But I don't plan on going camping again for a long, long time. I'm staying in my own bed at home where it's safe!"

Cody returned home tired from her exciting trip, and eager to see her mom and sister and talk to her dad on the phone. After she'd started her laundry, put away her things, and called her dad, she headed downstairs for dinner.

⟡🖐✍✍ ✍✍✍ ✍✍✍✍ ✍✍✍⟡, her mother

asked, using sign language so that Cody's little sister, Tana, who was deaf, could be included in the conversation.

Code Buster's Key and Solution found on pp. 169, 177.

While Ms. Stadelhofer had explained what had happened on the trip to Mrs. Jones, Cody told her side of the story over spaghetti dinner, avoiding the dangerous parts so her mom wouldn't worry. Mrs. Jones was especially impressed that the Code Busters would be receiving a commendation.

Tana loved the pirate bookmark Cody bought her—Cody had bought four of the colorful bookmarks, one for each family member, as a reminder of the fun adventure she'd had.

"Any homework?" Mrs. Jones asked.

"Oh, yeah! Ms. Stad gave us a new code to solve."

Mrs. Jones smiled at Cody. "That should be easy for you and your Code Buster friends."

"Except this one is in hieroglyphics. We're going to a museum soon to see some Egyptian artifacts. Ms. Stad says there are all kinds of messages and codes hidden in art."

Cody got out the assignment sheet and showed the hieroglyphics to her mom.

"Have you decoded it?" her mom asked.

"Yes, but I don't know what it means," Cody said, showing her the answer.

Code Buster's Key and Solution found on pp. 172, 177.

"Hmmm," her mom said. "Another mystery for you to solve!"

"I know!" Cody exclaimed. "Ancient Egyptians used hieroglyphics, which are like codes. It seems like there are codes everywhere, even throughout history. I guess it's up to us to crack them, right?"

Key Book
&
Solutions

Morse Code:

A .-	H	O ---	V ...-
B -...	I ..	P .--.	W .--
C -.-.	J .---	Q --.-	X -..-
D -..	K -.-	R .-.	Y -.--
E .	L .-..	S ...	Z --..
F ..-.	M --	T -	
G --.	N -.	U ..-	

Orienteering Code:

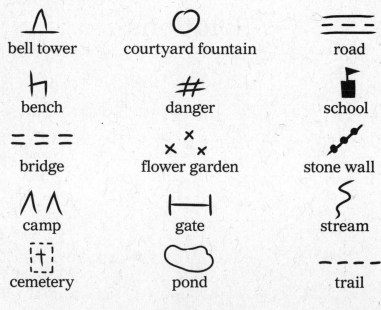

bell tower

courtyard fountain

road

bench

danger

school

bridge

flower garden

stone wall

camp

gate

stream

cemetery

pond

trail

166

Trail Signs Code:

	straight ahead	turn right	turn left	do not go this way
Stones				
Pebbles				
Twigs				
Long Grass				

Phonetic Alphabet:

A = Alpha

B = Bravo

C = Charlie

D = Delta

E = Echo

F = Foxtrot

G = Golf

H = Hotel

I = India

J = Juliet

K = Kilo

L = Lima

M = Mike

N = November

O = Oscar

P = Papa

Q = Quebec

R = Romeo

S = Sierra

T = Tango

U = Uniform

V = Victor

W = Whisker

X = X-ray

Y = Yankee

Z = Zulu

Caesar's Cipher:

A	B	C	D	E	F	G	H
Z	A	L	V	D	P	M	J

I	J	K	L	M	N	O	P
X	F	N	W	O	R	B	K

Q	R	S	T	U	V	W	X	Y	Z
S	C	I	U	Q	E	H	T	G	Y

Semaphore Code:

a b c d e f g h i

j k l m n o p q r

s t u v w x y z

Finger Spelling:

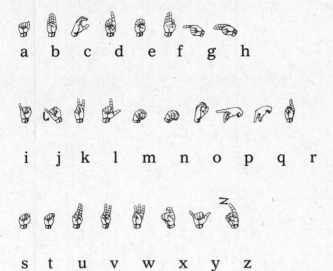

a b c d e f g h

i j k l m n o p q r

s t u v w x y z

Periodic Table Code:

Group	Z	Symbol	Name	Atomic Mass
1 (IA/1A)	1	H	Hydrogen	1.008
2 (IIA/2A)	3	Li	Lithium	6.941
2 (IIA/2A)	4	Be	Beryllium	9.012
1 (IA/1A)	11	Na	Sodium	22.990
2 (IIA/2A)	12	Mg	Magnesium	24.305
1 (IA/1A)	19	K	Potassium	39.098
2 (IIA/2A)	20	Ca	Calcium	40.078
3 (IIIB/3B)	21	Sc	Scandium	44.956
4 (IVB/4B)	22	Ti	Titanium	47.88
5 (VB/5B)	23	V	Vanadium	50.942
6 (VIB/6B)	24	Cr	Chromium	51.996
7 (VIIB/7B)	25	Mn	Manganese	54.938
8 (VIII/8)	26	Fe	Iron	55.933
9 (VIII/8)	27	Co	Cobalt	58.933
10 (VIII)	28	Ni	Nickel	58.693
11 (IB/1B)	29	Cu	Copper	63.546
12 (IIB/2B)	30	Zn	Zinc	65.39
13 (IIIA/3A)	5	B	Boron	10.811
13 (IIIA/3A)	13	Al	Aluminum	26.982
13 (IIIA/3A)	31	Ga	Gallium	69.732
14 (IVA/4A)	6	C	Carbon	12.011
14 (IVA/4A)	14	Si	Silicon	28.086
14 (IVA/4A)	32	Ge	Germanium	72.61
15 (VA/5A)	7	N	Nitrogen	14.007
15 (VA/5A)	15	P	Phosphorus	30.974
15 (VA/5A)	33	As	Arsenic	74.922
16 (VIA/6A)	8	O	Oxygen	15.999
16 (VIA/6A)	16	S	Sulfur	32.066
16 (VIA/6A)	34	Se	Selenium	78.09
17 (VIIA/7A)	9	F	Fluorine	18.998
17 (VIIA/7A)	17	Cl	Chlorine	35.453
17 (VIIA/7A)	35	Br	Bromine	79.904
18 (VIIIA/8A)	2	He	Helium	4.003
18 (VIIIA/8A)	10	Ne	Neon	20.180
18 (VIIIA/8A)	18	Ar	Argon	39.948
18 (VIIIA/8A)	36	Kr	Krypton	84.80
1	37	Rb	Rubidium	84.468
2	38	Sr	Strontium	87.62
3	39	Y	Yttrium	88.906
4	40	Zr	Zirconium	91.224
5	41	Nb	Niobium	92.906
6	42	Mo	Molybdenum	95.94
7	43	Tc	Technetium	98.907
8	44	Ru	Ruthenium	101.07
9	45	Rh	Rhodium	102.906
10	46	Pd	Palladium	106.42
11	47	Ag	Silver	107.868
12	48	Cd	Cadmium	112.411
13	49	In	Indium	114.818
14	50	Sn	Tin	118.71
15	51	Sb	Antimony	121.760
16	52	Te	Tellurium	127.6
17	53	I	Iodine	126.904
18	54	Xe	Xenon	131.29
1	55	Cs	Cesium	132.905
2	56	Ba	Barium	137.327
3	57–71		Lanthanide Series	
4	72	Hf	Hafnium	178.49
5	73	Ta	Tantalum	180.948
6	74	W	Tungsten	183.85
7	75	Re	Rhenium	186.207
8	76	Os	Osmium	190.23
9	77	Ir	Iridium	192.22
10	78	Pt	Platinum	195.08
11	79	Au	Gold	196.967
12	80	Hg	Mercury	200.59
13	81	Tl	Thallium	204.383
14	82	Pb	Lead	207.2
15	83	Bi	Bismuth	208.980
16	84	Po	Polonium	[208.882]
17	85	At	Astatine	209.987
18	86	Rn	Radon	222.018
1	87	Fr	Francium	223.020
2	88	Ra	Radium	226.025
3	89–103		Actinide Series	
4	104	Rf	Rutherfordium	[261]
5	105	Db	Dubnium	[262]
6	106	Sg	Seaborgium	[266]
7	107	Bh	Bohrium	[264]
8	108	Hs	Hassium	[269]
9	109	Mt	Meitnerium	[268]
10	110	Ds	Darmstadtium	[269]
11	111	Rg	Roentgenium	[272]
12	112	Cn	Copernicium	[277]
13	113	Uut	Ununtrium	unknown
14	114	Fl	Flerovium	[289]
15	115	Uup	Ununpentium	unknown
16	116	Lv	Livermorium	[298]
17	117	Uus	Ununseptium	unknown
18	118	Uuo	Ununoctium	unknown

Lanthanide Series

Z	Symbol	Name	Atomic Mass
57	La	Lanthanum	138.906
58	Ce	Cerium	140.115
59	Pr	Praseodymium	140.908
60	Nd	Neodymium	144.24
61	Pm	Promethium	144.913
62	Sm	Samarium	150.36
63	Eu	Europium	151.966
64	Gd	Gadolinium	157.25
65	Tb	Terbium	158.925
66	Dy	Dysprosium	162.50
67	Ho	Holmium	164.930
68	Er	Erbium	167.26
69	Tm	Thulium	168.934
70	Yb	Ytterbium	173.04
71	Lu	Lutetium	174.967

Actinide Series

Z	Symbol	Name	Atomic Mass
89	Ac	Actinium	227.028
90	Th	Thorium	232.038
91	Pa	Protactinium	231.036
92	U	Uranium	238.029
93	Np	Neptunium	237.048
94	Pu	Plutonium	244.064
95	Am	Americium	243.061
96	Cm	Curium	247.070
97	Bk	Berkelium	247.070
98	Cf	Californium	251.080
99	Es	Einsteinium	[254]
100	Fm	Fermium	257.095
101	Md	Mendelevium	258.1
102	No	Nobelium	259.101
103	Lr	Lawrencium	[282]

Reverse Alphabet Code:

A	B	C	D	E	F	G	H	I	J	K	L	M
Z	Y	X	W	V	U	T	S	R	Q	P	O	N

N	O	P	Q	R	S	T	U	V	W	X	Y	Z
M	L	K	J	I	H	G	F	E	D	C	B	A

Alphanumeric Code (2):

All around the mulberry bush
1 2 3 4 5 6 7 8 9 10 11 12 13 14 15 16 17 18 19 20 21 22 23 24

The monkey chased the weasel
1 2 3 4 5 6 7 8 9 10 11 12 13 14 15 16 17 18 19 20 21 22 23 24

The monkey thought twas all in fun
1 2 3 4 5 6 7 8 9 10 11 12 13 14 15 16 17 18 19 20 21 22 23 24 25 26 27 28

Pop goes the weasel
1 2 3 4 5 6 7 8 9 10 11 12 13 14 15 16

Egyptian Hieroglyphic Alphabet:

A 𓅃	H 𓉔	O 𓂝	V 𓅂
B 𓃀	I 𓇋	P 𓊪	W 𓏏
C 𓎡	J 𓆓	Q 𓈎	X 𓎡𓊃
D 𓂧	K 𓎡	R 𓂋	Y 𓏭
E 𓂋	L 𓃭	S 𓋴	Z 𓊃
F 𓆑	M 𓅓	T 𓏏	
G 𓎼	N 𓈖	U 𓅱	

Chapter 1

Caesar's cipher:

I wonder if there's a pirate code?

Hidden Word Search Puzzle:

C	P	I	R	A	T	E	S	A	M
A	B	C	D	E	F	G	E	H	I
R	I	J	V	K	L	M	A	N	S
M	O	P	I	W	H	E	R	E	S
E	Q	R	S	S	T	U	C	V	I
L	W	X	I	Y	Z	A	H	B	O
W	A	N	T	S	C	D	E	E	N
H	F	F	G	H	I	J	D	K	L
O	O	M	N	T	H	E	O	P	Q
T	R	E	A	S	U	R	E	R	S

WHO WANTS TO VISIT THE CARMEL MISSION
WHERE PIRATES SEARCHED FOR TREASURE?

Chapter 2

Morse code: **DJ, ME**

Backward code: **Monday**

Orienteering code:

ca=camp, po=pond, st=stream, br=bridge, ro=road, ga=gate, be=bench, tr=trail, Au=gold, Ag=silver

Direction code: **Go northwest, 10 steps, turn right, make a U-turn, go left 90 degrees.**

Chapter 3

Orienteering symbol code:

1. Find your TENT and set up. 2. Gather at the beginning of the TRAIL. 3. As you walk, watch for hidden messages near each BENCH. 4. Gather at the GATE. 5. Keep an eye out for DANGER!

Chapter 4

Trail signs code: **Right; do not go this way; left; straight ahead; do not go this way; right; left.**
Trail riddle: **Pop Goes the Weasel**

Chapter 5

Morse code:

1. Hi there!

2. Stop!

3. To cheat.

4. Pirate flag. – (Jolly Roger actually means "pretty red," and features a skull and crossbones.)

5. To speak. (Also to have a conversation or settle a dispute.)

6. Wow!

7. Pirate.

8. Person on land. (One who does not belong at sea.)

9. Chicken eggs.

10. Bottom of sea.

Pig Latin: **We need to see that map!**

<u>Chapter 6</u>

Finger spelling: **Stay here.**

Nursery rhyme code: **<u>All</u> I can find <u>around</u> this place is <u>the</u> path made of <u>cobbler's</u> stone. There's a <u>bench</u> that's carved with <u>the</u> form of a <u>monkey</u> that I have <u>chased</u> until I've tired. <u>The</u> only friend a <u>weasel</u> who thinks I'm <u>the</u> one acting the <u>monkey,</u> but my own <u>thought</u> is, that soon <u>it</u> will I hope <u>all</u> be worth it. <u>In</u> fact, though not <u>fun,</u> I shall see <u>Pop</u> when the man <u>goes</u> with me into <u>the</u> mouth of the <u>weasel</u>.**

All around the cobbler's bench the monkey chased the weasel. The monkey thought it all in fun. Pop goes the weasel.

Reverse alphabet code: **This is so fun!**

I want to be a pirate!

Chapter 7

Semaphore code: **Cool.**

Phonetic alphabet code: **Look!**

Where?

Them!

'Sup?

Morse code: **Did you find map?**

Chapter 8

Morse code: **Found map. Head back.**

Text message translations: **"Are you sending code?" "No, thought you were." "What's up?" "I don't know. Something about a map." "We'll check it out tomorrow. Later."**

Orienteering code: **flower garden, courtyard fountain, bell tower, stone wall, cemetery, school**

Finger spelling: **Quiet**

Listen

Follow her

Chapter 9

Marine flag code: **Help!**

Morse code: **Careful**

Chapter 10

Alphanumeric code: **Treasure at museum.**

Chapter 11

Mirror code: Hold the code up to a mirror and read
the message in the reflection:

Make new friends,

But keep the old.

One is silver,

And the other gold.

Chapter 12

Finger spelling: **How was your trip?**

Egyptian hieroglyphics: **steganography**

Finger Spelling:
Chapter Title Translations

Chapter 1 *A Pirate in California*

Chapter 2 *M Is for Map*

Chapter 3 *Following Clues*

Chapter 4 *A Puzzle Within a Puzzle*

Chapter 5 *Mystery of the Mission*

Chapter 6 *Pop Goes the Puzzle*

Chapter 7 *Longbeard and Jolly*

Chapter 8 *A Flash in the Night*

Chapter 9 *The Lost Treasure*

Chapter 10 *Avast, Ye Sea Dogs!*

Chapter 11 *Who Is Chad Bour?*

Chapter 12 *The Code Is Cracked!*

How to Make Your Own Invisible Ink

1. Lemon Juice
Write your message with lemon juice using a cotton swab on plain white paper. Let it dry, then send it to a friend and have him or her hold it over a lightbulb. The message will be revealed!

2. Milk
Instead of lemon juice, use milk. Follow the instructions above.

3. Baking Soda
Mix a few spoonfuls of baking soda with water to make a paste. Use a cotton swab to write your message. To read the message, hold the paper over a lightbulb or dip a cotton swab in grape juice and rub it over the paper.

4. White Crayon
Write a message on white paper with a white crayon. Have your friend color over the paper with a marker to see the secret message.

5. Banana
Write a message on a banana peel with a toothpick. About an hour later, the message will magically appear.

Suggestions for How Teachers Can Use the Code Busters Club Series in the Classroom

Kids love codes. They will want to "solve" the codes in this novel before looking up the solutions. This means they will be practicing skills that are necessary to their class work in several courses, but in a non-pressured way.

The codes in this book vary in level of difficulty, so there is something for students of every ability. The codes move from a simple code wheel—a Caesar's cipher wheel—to more widely accepted "code" languages such as Morse code and semaphore.

In a mathematics classroom, the codes in this book can easily be used as motivational devices to teach problem-solving and reasoning skills. Both of these have become important elements in the curriculum at all grade levels. The emphasis throughout the book on regarding codes as *patterns* gives students a great deal of practice in one of the primary strategies of problem solving. The strategy of "Looking for a Pattern" is basic to much of mathematics. The resolving of codes demonstrates how important patterns are. These codes can lead to discussions of the logic behind why they "work" (problem solving). The teacher can then have the students create their own codes (problem formulation) and try sending secret messages to one another, while other students try to "break the code." Developing and resolving these new codes will require a great deal of careful reasoning on the part of the students. The class might also wish to do some practical research in statistics, to determine which letters occur most frequently in the English language. (*E*, *T*, *A*, *O*, and *N* are the five most widely used letters, and should appear most often in coded messages.)

This book may also be used in other classroom areas of study, such as social studies, with its references to the California mission system, messages hidden in rhyme, and codes employed during wartime. This book raises questions such as, "Why would semaphore be important today? Where is it still used?"

In the English classroom, spelling is approached as a "deciphering code." The teacher may also suggest the students do some outside reading. They might read a biography of Samuel Morse or Louis Braille, or even the Sherlock Holmes mystery "The Adventure of the Dancing Men."

This book also refers to modern texting on cell phones and computers as a form of code. Students could explain what the various "code" abbreviations they use mean today and why they are used.   —*Dr. Stephen Krulik*

Dr. Stephen Krulik has a distinguished career as a professor of mathematics education. Professor emeritus at Temple University, he received the 1721 Lifetime Achievement Award from the National Council of Teachers of Mathematics.

ACKNOWLEDGMENTS

Thanks to Colleen Casey, Janet Finsilver, Staci McLaughlin, Ann Parker, and Carole Price for their expertise. Thanks to the Spy Museum in Washington, D.C. And a special thanks to Code Busters Club members: Avery Aplanalp, Jack Borovitz, Connor Brien, Erin Casey, Tara Casey, Sydney Closson, Isha Desai, Mikayla Freeman, Joshua Frendberg, Sequoia Hack, Melissa Hernandez, Ryan Hillary, Ty Littlefield, Courtney Lyons, Jake McLaughlin, Jodie Pike, Miranda Stewart, Lauren Strong, and Shaun Woods.

Keep cracking codes in

The
CODE BUSTERS
CLUB

CASE #4:

The Mummy's
Curse

Available from Egmont USA Fall 2014

Chapter 1

"I give up!" Cody said to her mother as she entered the breakfast nook before school Monday morning. Cody bounded into the room dressed in a yellow short-sleeved T-shirt that set off her curly red ponytail. Well-worn jeans and a pair of red Converse Chucks completed her simple outfit. Lately the spring weather had been so sunny, all she'd need was her red hoodie and she'd be set for the short walk to Berkeley Cooperative Middle School.

"What's the matter?" Mrs. Jones asked her

thirteen-year-old daughter, before sipping from a mug of hot, steaming coffee. Already dressed in her uniform, Cody's mother was ready for her job at the Berkeley Police Department. "Did you have trouble figuring out the puzzle Ms. Stadelhofer gave you for homework?"

"No," Cody said and signed, so her deaf four-year-old sister, Tana, would be included in the conversation. "That was pretty easy." She sat down on a stool, filled her bowl with Cheerios, her favorite cereal since she was little, and added milk. "We've been studying ancient Egypt in class, and Ms. Stad gave us these cool decoder cards that have the Egyptian hieroglyphic alphabet, so I knew that was the key." She took a spoonful of cereal.

"What mean h-i-r-o . . . ?" Tana tried to finger-spell the word.

Code Buster's Key and Solution found on pp. 169, 191.

Cody slowly respelled the word using the American Sign Language manual alphabet, then signed,

"Hieroglyphs are like words and stories written in pictures."

She turned to her mother. "We're going to the Rosicrucian Egyptian Museum in San Jose on Friday to see some hieroglyphs and ancient artifacts, and even a mummy." Cody had never seen a mummy before, except in movies, and *they* always looked fake. She wondered if she'd be creeped out by a real one.

"So what's the problem?" her mother asked.

"I'm not sure what Ms. Stad's word means." Cody took out the assignment from her backpack and showed it to her mom. Written underneath the hieroglyphic symbols was Cody's English translation.

Code Buster's Key and Solution found on pp. 172, 191.

Cody's mom looked at the decoded word her daughter had written. "Did you look it up?"

"The dictionary says it means 'concealed writing'—kind of like a hidden message. But that's all I know."

"Hmm," her mom murmured. "It sounds like Ms. Stadelhofer has another mysterious puzzle for you to solve."

"Seriously! I hope there are a bunch of hidden messages at the museum. Ms. Stad said the place is full of mysteries. She said to make sure we study our latest spelling words, because they'll be part of our assignment. I have a feeling she's making up some puzzles for us, too."

"Sounds fun. Do you want me to quiz you?" Cody's mother asked.

"Sure." Cody handed the word list to her mother. Cody was a good speller. She'd taught herself tricks for remembering difficult words and almost always got 100 percent on her tests. But this time she might not do as well because these new words were so different. They were the names of Egyptian gods and goddesses.

As her mother read off each spelling word, Cody wrote it down on a piece of paper. Most of the names weren't too hard—*Amun, Anubis, Bastet, Horus, Isis, Osiris, Sekhmet, Sobek.* She could sound them out. But *Maat* was tricky—two *a*'s instead of two *t*'s like Matt the Brat. And *Thoth* was pronounced *toth*, so she had to remember to add the silent *h*.

"How'd I do?" she asked her mother after she'd corrected the test.

"Perfect, as usual," her mom said. "Do you have to know why all the gods and goddesses were worshipped? They each had their specific purposes."

"Yep, I memorized them, and we picked our favorites as our Egyptian Code Buster names," Cody replied. She began to recite: "Let's see. Amun was the god of air and invisibility. That's the one I chose, because I'd love to be invisible sometimes and just watch people. Anubis was the god of death. Bastet was the cat goddess. M.E. chose that one because she loves animals. Horus was the god of war and the sky. Isis was the goddess of magic. That's Quinn's favorite, since he's been learning magic tricks. Maat was the goddess of truth and justice. Osiris was the god of the underworld and afterlife. Sekhmet was the goddess of lions and power. That's Luke's Egyptian code name, because he's strong. Then there's

Sobek . . . Sobek . . . um . . ." Cody shook her head.

"I think he's the god of crocodiles," Mrs. Jones said.

"Right! Crocodiles," Cody said. "And the last one is Thoth, the god of wisdom. I just have to remember Sobek. Then I'll know them all!"

CODE BUSTER'S

Solutions

Chapter 1

Finger spelling: Chapter 1: *Eye Spy*

Finger spelling: **Hieroglyphic**

Egyptian hieroglyphics: **Steganography**